RVN

TIM GINGRAS

outskirts
press

Outskirts Press, Inc.
http://www.outskirtspress.com

Paperback ISBN: 978-1-9772-0133-1
Hardback ISBN: 978-1-9772-0231-4

Library of Congress Control Number: 2018908947

Cover Photo © 2018 www.gettyimages.com. All rights reserved - used with permission.

Outskirts Press and the "OP" logo are trademarks belonging to Outskirts Press, Inc.

PRINTED IN THE UNITED STATES OF AMERICA

Thank you

Mrs. Laurette Kittler for inspiring me in my youth to imagine, and embrace storytelling.

Mrs. Susan Giosa for inspiring me to look deep within myself, to create real characters, and to work hard.

Mr. Robert M. Heskett, who inspired me to become stronger by lifting heavier weights.

Also, thank you to Outskirts, JOKES4MILES, '77 Rowdies, and Dr. Roberto Coira.

Dedicated to:

The 58,202 US soldiers who were KIA/MIA due to "in-country" Vietnam war service; the 17,725 Vietnam War drafted KIA/MIA — not their choice, but these soldiers gave their full measure of devotion; and to nearly 10,000,000 who served during the Vietnam War era.

Author's Note

Author will dedicate 15% of all author's net royalties from every book sold to accredited veterans' organizations.

MY OLDER BROTHER'S grandson, J.D., is setting up his camera and lights in front of me. J.D. is in film school in Chicago, and he says this interview is important for his final grade before graduating college. I agreed to be here, and we discussed everything three weeks ago. I know what he wants, and I'm going to do my best for him. J.D. is a great kid, and he always has been. He got my older brother's "Smart DNA," that's for sure. His passion for excellence is impressive, and his attention to detail with this has been impressive. We have been here for almost an hour setting up. Seems like overkill to me, but I agreed to give him these few hours today. J.D. wants to interview me regarding my military service and Vietnam. I agreed to only discuss what happened from the time I turned eighteen, on January 3, 1966, to June 1968, when I got my DD-214 with the Honorable Discharge on it. Nothing beyond that. The kid has said that's exactly what he wants, and he understands my schedule is confined to three hours today. He's a good kid.

After about an hour of setup, he finally sits down across from me with all his notes. He asks his crew of three people if everyone is ready. They all say, "Ready," so J.D. simply says,

"Let's begin." We had agreed that he would ask me the first question on camera, using one camera on him, and the other camera would switch to me for my response.

I say, "J.D., let's light this candle."

He leans forward and says, "Roll please." He speaks to the camera and introduces himself and gives a brief explanation to the camera behind me.

"I'm sitting here with Charles 'Charlie' Kinane, and he is a veteran of the Vietnam War. Charlie is also my great-uncle, and I want to thank him in advance for agreeing to share his military experience. Thank you, Uncle Charlie. This means a lot to me, and I'm sure from what I understand, your experience is fascinating. We understand you've never really spoken of your Vietnam experience. We appreciate your time and candor, Uncle Charlie."

"You're welcome, J.D."

"Please begin with your name, when you were born, and begin telling your story anytime you're ready. If we need a break, we'll break, and if I need to ask a question, I will," J.D. explains.

"Okay, Roger that." I am ready, so I look right into the camera behind J.D. as he instructed earlier.

MY NAME IS Charles (Charlie) Kinane. I was born in Chicago on January 3, 1948. I am currently over seventy years old, and I feel it's time I tell you what happened during my military experience, which includes my tour in-country, in Vietnam (Republic of Vietnam or RVN). Certain things stay on your mind twenty-four/seven, and my RVN experiences, good and bad, are embedded in my mind. This memory is there in my dreams, when I wake up, during showers, throughout my day, and when I close my eyes and fall asleep at night, now that I can sleep again. I have never told anyone this entire story.

It started on my eighteenth birthday, January 3, 1966, which was our first day back from Christmas break. One of the high school counselors pulled me out of class to tell me something very important. The counselor seemed to be a decent man in his fifties, I guess. He told me that it was important for him to tell me personally that I must register for the draft as soon as I could. It was the law, and he said he did this with each male student who turned eighteen while in school. He said it was the policy of the school. He also took that time to inform me that based on my grades, and since my older brother was doing well in college and riding a deferment, "You're probably going to get drafted, Charlie. Be prepared for that after graduation. You're welcome to come to my office anytime you want," and he turned around to walk away. He left me there thinking, *That was weird*. Primarily, because I had never been brought out of class like that, and he seemed so serious.

I stood there for about fifteen minutes thinking about what he told me. It just seemed so strange, and I wasn't actually thinking about the draft thing. I snapped out of my deep thought when the bell rang and the class I was in dismissed. I went back to get my book and head to my next class that day.

That was my eighteenth birthday present, I thought. *Damn. I've got to figure this out.*

Just to tell you a little about me:

GROWING UP I enjoyed Chicago summers, and for the first time in my life, I thought I might not have that chance during the summer of 1966. Outdoor activities were always entertaining, with sixteen-inch softball, regular baseball, basketball, boxing, and hockey outside during winters, and swimming in Lake Michigan, along the rocks on the Northside of Chicago's Lake Front during summers. In high school, I ran cross country and track, and competed in many city, state, and regional meets. Running kept me in excellent shape and on time for early morning classes. I was eighteen years old and seemingly at the beginning of my physical peak.

Growing up in the Lakeview Neighborhood on the north side of Chicago near Wrigley Field, home of my favorite team, the Chicago Cubs, I recall hearing the roar of the crowds throughout each summer at Wrigley Field, and occasionally going to a game. Tickets were not that expensive and usually plentiful for each home game. I recall "Ladies Day" almost every Thursday, and WGN-TV & Radio broadcasts of games with the voice of the Cubs, Jack Brickhouse. The smells of the ball park were as familiar and wonderfully reliable to the sense of smell as any, with smells of hot dogs, onions, and beer. It was a very unique neighborhood to grow up in, but not without its problems, and there were land mines in terms of run-down buildings, homes, and rough characters seemingly around every corner. Learning those Wrigley Field area streets simply to survive sometimes probably came in handy throughout my service, and my entire life, yet the fond memories of youth far outweighed the negatives.

I recall the occasional date with a high school gal I met during junior year. Movies, burgers, tennis, walks, bike rides, when off time from some high school kid job permitted. I guess I could say I was a good-looking kid, and my being raised to be courteous and polite scored additional points with all women. I knew I was charming and funny because I was always told that by friends and family. Even though all the high school gals I dated were wonderful on many levels, having a "steady" girlfriend just didn't seem to fit into my routine. At eighteen, and with what was happening in the world at that time, I felt there would be plenty of time to meet someone to get close to emotionally. Those considerations seemed years off for this boy, away in the future. Especially in light of the likelihood of me being drafted and tangled up in this war somewhere in a place called Vietnam. As I said, I turned eighteen on January 3, 1966, and the United States was knee deep in this war. I knew of older friends who were already over there, dead, or injured badly. If I was going to become part of this mess, I would reluctantly serve my country if called, and simply try to survive. With all this weighing heavily on my mind at the end of my high school days, having a "steady" just didn't work for me.

My older (only) brother was riding a college deferment. To me, and others, he was basically a genius academically. Genius. As though simply having an older brother isn't enough pressure, mine is older and all-around incredible. Other friends were high school classmates, some neighborhood kids, a couple coworkers, and high school sports teammates. From time to time, I developed close friendships, but they always slipped away over time, or for various "growing-up" reasons. Different schools, moving away, going steady with a local girlfriend. I did find plenty of time to be alone and enjoy wholesome independence. I spent many weekend evenings drinking a couple of beers at "The Rocks" along Chicago Lakefront; even though beer was prohibited in the parks, I would sneak in a couple of large cans of beer I was somehow able to buy at this little mom-and-pop grocery store. Friends weren't always necessary for me to enjoy quiet evenings and a slight beer buzz many Saturday nights along Lake Michigan.

High school graduation came fast, and before I knew it, it was June 1966, and I was graduating on time on the Northside of Chicago. Overall, during high school, I was a mediocre student. I wasn't dumb, but my attention would drift in and out of classroom work. I always seemed tired in class and rarely had enough time to complete assigned homework. Outside of class, I was active in sports and participated in social activities.

My immediate family struggled because my parents divorced early in my life. My extended family was strong—a solid Catholic family from Chicago. I had one sibling, my older brother, who I have already explained is much wiser than I'll ever be. At least during that time I knew in my heart I wasn't sure about college. I worked restaurant jobs to help pay for tuition at Catholic high school and contribute to the family budget, and I knew doing this type of honest work wasn't my goal. Even though I wasn't sure what my goals were at that time, I knew there was way more than this type of labor to make a living.

On June 8, 1966, one week after high school graduation, the notice came from the Selective Service System. My Order to Report for Induction. It had my name and address on it and the date I was to report. I had to read it over and over for hours. Even though I knew it was coming, I still could not believe I was being drafted. I had a feeling I would get drafted but anticipated a little more time to enjoy a simple life after high school, while trying to figure out a path for myself. I had less than sixty days to report for my physical and induction somewhere in downtown Chicago, The Loop. I recall walking around in a daze for a few days, and finally telling my mother.

Mom was upset and wanted me to find a way to a deferment. Father wasn't an issue, because he had gone back to Canada, where he was from, and we rarely saw him. I never understood the problems between my mom and dad, but he wasn't considered a nice person, so it simply wasn't discussed. Other family members were concerned and/or supportive. After the initial news of my draft, my family stopped talking about it. I guess I didn't want to think about it either anymore until the day before induction, and I really didn't. Grandparents and uncles had served, but now it was this generation, starting with me in my extended family being called to serve. Those in my family who had served never wanted to talk about their experience, and even though I would ask a question of them occasionally, they brushed my questions off with "That was a long time ago," which made me believe in my heart, it wasn't a good experience for them. I wasn't so much upset as I was really concerned about this, and frankly scared.

My Options:

AFTER WAKING UP from a daze about a week later, I started to figure out I may have options. I honestly don't know who I heard this from, but I know I heard it. Prior to reporting for induction physical, I could possibly choose to enlist in the Navy or Air Force. I was trying to hedge my bet in order to survive my active duty service. I recall going to the recruitment office on Irving Park Road, near Lincoln Avenue on the northwest side of Chicago. I remember being extremely intimidated by the guys in uniforms. Opening the big door and walking into this older building with arching marble walls and ceilings, I took about ten steps towards the Navy office and stopped in front where they had a rack on the wall with brochures and a soft-covered guide to all the jobs in the Navy. As the petty officer was approaching me, I just said hi and told him I would read this and try to come back for questions. He greeted me enthusiastically, and insisted I take his card. I grabbed it, looked at his name, and said thank you…I was about to say mister, or sir, but I couldn't figure out would be right. Nobody knew I was doing this, and I really felt intimidated, yet still in awe.

I remember trying to read everything I could about all the different career paths you can choose. I didn't bounce this off anyone, and I didn't seek anyone's opinion. Perhaps at eighteen, I should have, but I felt pretty good at that time: I was potentially making the right move so I could serve—and survive.

It seemed like almost all the jobs in the Navy at that time involved getting dirty all the time, and exposed to loud noises all the time, while living in very cramped quarters ALL THE TIME. I'm not sure why I landed on Navy corpsman, but I did because the job description said I could be assigned to an environment that is extremely clean and sanitary, or the exact opposite. Huh, again I was trying to hedge my bet to survive this military service obligation I was willing to fulfill, and from what I had seen on the nightly news, nothing looked clean or sanitary where the combat was, so perhaps that meant serving here in the States at some naval hospital. I read "Exact Opposite," but because there seemed to be a better chance to survive this call to duty with this choice, I had to think about it for a day or two.

Two days later, I was back. I walked to the door of the U.S. Navy Recruitment office inside that echoing old and cold marble interior. The same guy greeted me again. "Hey, good to see you again. Are you really interested in the Navy? My name is Petty Officer…" He mumbled some long name I didn't remember right after he said it directly to me, while shaking my hand with a big grin. I even looked at his name tag, and it was a very long name, and I wondered *How did they fit all those letters on that tag?*

I don't recall the entire meeting, other than filling out some forms, and that seemed to take an hour or two. I had mentioned that I had just graduated at the high school four blocks away, and he dropped one of the counselor's names on me, and I said, "Oh, yeah, I know him." Small talk. He offered me a Coke, and I accepted while completing the forms. I realized after I said sure to the drink, he seemed disappointed that I accepted for some reason. I think he wanted to keep his supply for himself, but was encouraged to offer a beverage to eighteen-year-old kids like me filling out forms. I think he said, "You're making my job easy, Charlie." I didn't voice my inner motive for joining, but I was certainly making this enlistment credit easy for him. He did say to me very seriously: "Charlie, please know I will convey in writing all I can with respect to your training wishes, but I can't 100 percent guarantee anything beyond basic training. The Navy's pretty good at spotting recruits who are sharp, dedicated, and work hard as a team, but this guidance will be duly noted in your official jacket."

I made my choice that day. At the end of forms, and some additional vague insight from the petty officer, I left with instructions to return the next day with my high school diploma. My first military assignment, I thought. A mission. My first orders.

THAT SAME AFTERNOON, I recall asking my Burger Ville boss if I could only work Saturday and Sunday evenings until I went into the military. He never spoke much, but he immediately understood, and knew there were dozens of neighborhood kids in line for my regular forty-hour evenings job. It was a small stand he built from scratch, and his business was busy all the time, especially on weekend nights. He was always up to code with the city and the county, while always willing to give local cops complimentary (bribes) hot dogs. It was "good business," he always said, so I ended up making a lot of friends with hungry local coppers. This strategy for surviving those streets of Chicago seemed to act as an insurance policy. The coolest part was what he paid. He ONLY accepted people recommended by a current employee. Shrewd, because he knew that the new guy was on whoever recommended someone bad. He also paid the best for this type of work, and he paid in cash, which made life easier too. He was a secretive, small, thin man with a beatnik type of beard. He seemed to live mysteriously somewhere nearby within Chicago's Gold Coast community, which meant to me he was rich. Carried a lot of cash too, and late at night. I'm sure he was packing. He was cool, because back in 1966, minimum wage was $1.25/hour. My Burger Ville boss paid three bucks an hour. Big difference and the only reason I could cut back on hours for the summer before becoming a U.S. Navy sailor. Rush & Oak on a Saturday during that time was amazing. So many people. A cool "going nowhere" part-time job.

So, now I've graduated high school, and technically avoided being drafted, enlisting in an effort to serve, but trying to wiggle around going to that mess building up over in Vietnam. The boss seemed quietly impressed. I felt gained some respect and a break from my enigma Burger Ville boss. In less than two months, I was going to take this to the next level and figure out a way to survive my call to service by my country. Vietnam was raging, and older guys I knew were dying over there, wherever that place was. Near Hawaii, I presumed. I had never been on a plane, let alone to Hawaii. I had one more big call to make before giving a copy of my high school diploma to Petty Officer "what's his name."

JUNE 8, 1966, I walked back into the recruitment center on Irving Park Road, near Damen and Lincoln, with my newly minted high school diploma in hand. I saw the same petty officer again, but this time, he was in a different Navy uniform. First time I saw him, he had a black uniform on, and now, this time, he was wearing a very bright, crispy white Cracker Jack type of uniform. He seemed very happy to see me as planned. He greeted me and said how much he appreciated me keeping my word and returning as I said I would with the diploma. He immediately removed the paper part from the slick leather binder so he could make a copy. That took him at least two minutes while I just stood there. When he had a good copy, he returned the certificate to me, and I put it back into the binder while he was talking. He asked me if I wanted a soda. I said another Coke would be great. He pulled it out of a cooler near his big metal government desk.

I don't think I'll ever remember his name, but the petty officer, now in white uniform, asked me to sit across from him. He seemed happy while closely looking at the certificate and congratulating me. He picked up a folder that I assume was filled with all the information on me, and stuck the copy into the folder. He pulled out another form and said, "Let's pick your A-School for training after basic training, and then we will pick your basic training location. Have you thought about what job training and job you want in the Navy?"

"I have," I responded. I was thinking I probably did more research on this over the last twenty-four hours than anyone else who had come to this desk in the last few months. He reminded me, before I answered, that he could ONLY get me assigned to A-School as long as I did well in Basic. That made sense, but I had another question: "What about C-School training beyond A-School?"

He said, "Nobody's ever asked me that, but what I can do is this. First, tell me what A-School you're interested in, and we'll discuss what I can do, or not be able to do, for C-Schools."

I told him I had been focusing on being a Navy corpsman and then going to Pharmacy Tech C-School. He leaned back in his chair and rubbed his crew-cut with both hands, back and forth. He was clearly thinking about this, while seeming to be slightly surprised by my request. As he straightened up his desk, he said, "That's a good choice for a C-School, and I see here on your application that you worked in a pharmacy down the road. Was that a good experience for you, Charlie?"

"It was only a part-time job two days a week, and I quit when I was about fifteen because I could make more money at the Burger Ville stand at Rush & Oak, but I did like the job. Mostly deliveries and stocking," I explained.

He seemed to give my request a lot of thought. Five minutes of watching him ponder seemed like a long time. Then he took a swig from his Coke can and spoke to me in a very serious tone. "I admire your thought process, Charlie, and this is what I will do." He repeated what he said the previous day. I actually appreciated it, and was able to look him straight in the eye, man to man. He knew I was listening. "First off, I can only 'guarantee,'" while he made those quotes with his fingers about shoulder level, "that you will get to basic training, and as long as you do well in Basic, you'll get your Corpsman A-School, but this is the only thing I can actually guarantee. Beyond A-School, all I can do is note and recommend that you want to serve in the Navy as a corpsman and hope to receive further training as a pharmacy tech, which is a C-School. You may get it right away or later down the road or maybe not at all. There are many factors that go into C-School assignments and opportunities in the Navy at the C-School level." He repeated the quotes sign with his fingers. "Does that make sense?"

I had to think for a moment. "So, as long as I do okay in Basic, I will be guaranteed Corpsman A-School?"

He said, "Yes, absolutely, you have my word on this."

"No B.S.? You WILL make your notes in my file as to this conversation and your recommendation?" I asked again.

"Absolutely. I will have you read everything I have just written down."

"Yes, thank you, I would like to read what you write."

He began typing on some official form he pulled out of the lower left-hand side of the desk. He didn't seem to be the fastest typist in the world, but I was grateful for what appeared to be his effort to make me a happy recruit. I sat there for about ten minutes until he was finished. He peeled the form out of the old manual typewriter, looked at it carefully, and handed it to me. As I reached for the form, I was thinking, *If this is right, this is my path, and I think I will survive this service requirement. I might just avoid Vietnam.* The form was in triplicate with carbon paper in the middle. He asked me to handle it carefully because of the carbon paper; otherwise, it would smudge all over. I held the freshly typed form around the edges, lightly in both hands, allowing it to rest in my lap. I read it very carefully twice. It wasn't a lot to read, but reading it twice gave me some form of comfort for some reason. Just as I was about to hand it back to the petty officer, I noticed the date read 8-May-1966. It was June 8th, so I asked him to make the correction and let me know where to sign. He tried to change it, but didn't like how it looked and said he wanted to always be "squared away," so he tore up that form and pulled out a fresh duplicate form.

While he was re-typing the form, I stayed quiet and simply looked around. There were three similar desks in this room that were empty. There were windows that looked into other recruitment offices. Army, Marine, and Air Force. Each office occupied by one person in uniform sitting at a desk and on the phone. I remember thinking about their uniforms and wondering how old they might be. All these recruiter guys in uniform seemed several years older than I was. I wondered how they really felt about their service. The petty officer had said he knew everyone in the building, but that people come and go. "That's how the military is," he said. "Beaucoup travel." I wasn't sure what that word meant, but it seemed like a lot.

After I gawked around my seat, he finished and ripped the form out of the old typewriter and looked at it, comparing it to the first form. "Here you go, Charlie," he said. I asked to compare both too, and he passed the first form over. They were the same, word for word, and the date was correct. I said, "Where do I sign?" He pointed to the line, and said to include today's date next to my signature. I signed quickly.

Then he asked me where I wanted to go to basic training and when. The date had to be prior to August 19, 1966, because my new report date officially had to be prior to the report date on my letter from Induction Services. I said, "Can I report on August 18th?"

He looked at his calendar and said, "That's a good date. That's a Thursday, which is perfect. Be prepared very early in the morning. We will send you a letter about a week prior to August 18th, with a specific time to pick you up. The letter will advise you of everything to bring with you, and I remind you to be outside your home five minutes prior to pickup time. If I need anything else from you, I will call. If you have any questions at all, you call me, or come into this office, okay?" I stood up, shook his hand, and thanked him for his time. He said, "Welcome to the United States, Navy Corpsman."

As I was shaking his hand, I made an eye-to-eye connection with him again and said, "Did you say Orlando was the only one of three Navy basic training bases?"

He said, "Yes."

"Did you also say Orlando is the only NBTB that trains female recruits?"

He said, "Roger that" in a very direct, but respectful way. I trusted this guy for some reason. I barely knew him, but I was putting the next few years into his hands today.

I said, "Please assign me to NBTB Orlando, Florida."

"Aye, aye, Charlie."

I turned around and exited the building, completely blown away by what just happened.

I had the remainder of the day to myself, and it was only

10:15. Cubs game? Why not? Drysdale was on the mound for the Dodgers. Something to do before I told Mom later.

CUBS WON. I recall there were a little more than five thousand people at the game. Seats were easy to occupy. Cubs ended up having a pathetic season, winning less than sixty games with their new manager, Leo Durocher, but the team had promise, and I'll always be a Cubs fan.

Got home and told Mom about my day. It didn't seem she really knew how to react, but as I explained what and why, she seemed to understand. Mom was simple and a little timid, but she knew what was going on, and knew I got the draft notice. I explained that the reason I enlisted in Navy was to serve, and try to figure out a way to survive and possibly even avoid getting mixed up in Vietnam. I also explained that I would be getting great training, and that after serving, I would have my college paid for with GI Bill benefits. I explained that I didn't believe I was ready for college now, and I was healthy, so deferment was out of the question. I had found out that since my father was Canadian, and since my parents separated and he moved back up north, he had encouraged me to move up there to avoid this Vietnam mess. I wasn't going to move to Canada, which guys were doing at that time. I had given it almost constant thought since turning eighteen on January 3, 1966. I was going to serve, but try to hedge my bets to simply survive. Mom and I always watched the CBS evening news with Walter Cronkite, and we knew how bad this was over there in Vietnam.

After our brief discussion, we didn't talk for the remainder of that evening. The next day she broke the news to extended family. The hardest part of my decision to enlist seemed over for now. At least until August 18, 1966, when I had to report. I figured until then, I would enjoy this summer as much as I could. What a summer 1966 was too.

JUNE 9, 1966 was a sunny Thursday. I had seventy days to enjoy this final Chicago summer for a while. I only had to work shifts late on Saturdays and Sundays. Easy, and it gave me plenty of pocket money. I was going to try to really enjoy this summer. Swimming down by the lake. Golfing at Waveland Golf Course. Riding my bike. Seeing a movie here and there. Maybe a nice date. I remember walking only a few blocks to Lake Michigan, Montrose Harbor, and thinking, *It's going to be okay, Charlie... It's going to be okay*, and I convinced myself of that during the walk that day.

That summer was hot, and it didn't rain much at all. The lakefront at "The Rocks" on the north side and near Montrose Harbor was always packed. I rode my bike every day down near the lakefront. Foster Beach on Chicago's far north side to Oak Street Beach was a great bike ride. It was easy to jump off the bike almost anywhere along the lakefront and jump into the water for a swim.

I went to movies a few times a week. I recall seeing *Our Man Flint* several times and *Fantastic Voyage* a few times too. *The Russians Are Coming!* was funny too. I would typically go alone to either Riviera Theater or Uptown Theater; they were both close, and cheap compared to downtown theaters, and they always showed good movies. Tickets were fifty cents each during the week, and seventy-five cents on weekends. It was a great way to escape the heat and humidity, because the air-conditioning inside was always refreshing. I recall how humid it was the moment you opened the big glass doors of the theater to walk on the street. The humidity was so over-whelming at times, it felt like walking through an unseen shower. As soon as you hit the street, your clothes were im-mediately wet, and sweating would start.

I also went to Riverview Amusement park a couple of times. Riverview was a great place to have fun if you had a few bucks in your pocket. It was near Lane Tech High School, so I had to take a Chicago bus. The buses were usually trolley buses, where the bus was hooked up to some electric cables above it. The buses always ran, but occasionally, and I'm not sure why, the cables would detach from the cable, and the bus would simply shut down. The bus driver would quickly get out of his seat, open the front door, and walk outside the bus towards the back, and somehow reattach the bus to the cable. The few times I saw this, everyone on the bus seemed fas-cinated and briefly entertained by the uniformed bus driver mumbling to himself as he got the bus hooked up again. It always seemed to be a quick fix, because it only took the bus driver a couple of minutes to get us back and running. The bus ride to Riverview took about fifteen minutes.

Riverview had great rides: the Bobs, which was the big roller coaster; the Shoots, which was a ride where you were actually in a boat, and you would go down a slide and land in some water, and the splash would soak all on board. The parachute drop was popular, but I wasn't particularly fond of heights and not interested in this type of amusement. There were games of skill and chance, and great carnival-type food at Riverview. I never went at night, because I had heard people were being mugged going into or leaving Riverview, so I thought daytime was plenty of fun, and less of a hassle with punks — and let me tell you, there were always gangs of troublemaking punks around. The trick was to avoid them at all costs, and I did.

That summer was also when Martin Luther King Jr. was in town marching and protesting for civil rights. I recall from the evening news that he gave a big address to a full house at Soldier Field that summer. Each nightly newscast seemed to suggest that Mayor Richard J. Daley didn't enjoy having MLK in town and seemed grumpy about those Freedom Marches almost every day. There were fights and riots all over town that summer. Especially on the south side of the city. There was one big riot one night at Division and Damen that got a lot of attention. The National Guard was around Chicago that summer and had actually made a campsite out of one of the local parks. Clarendon Park, not too far from where we lived, was one of those parks. I saw big tents and many vehicles taking over the ball fields for weeks. I would see this when I rode my bike towards the lakefront, and it seemed surreal. I wondered if this is what it looked like in Vietnam.

The biggest news in Chicago that summer came after July 14th. Those young nursing students all living together on the far south side of Chicago were murdered by that evil Richard Speck. It became big news for a few days because of how gruesome and random the murders seemed to be, and also because it took a few days before they found Speck in some Madison Avenue flophouse. There were many flophouses in Chicago. They were typically older hotels that were quite run-down, but still offered rooms for rent. Basically, bare bones, and a place to sleep. Very poor people usually stayed or lived there. It was basically skid row in Chicago. After about three days, they found Speck in one of these old hotels on Madison Avenue, and it seemed as though the entire city was able to breathe a sigh of relief he was caught. He seemed like a real creep, and quite evil to do what he did. I thought about the young Filipino nursing student who was able to hide and avoid being one of those victims. I thought how brave she was and how terrified she must have been. They were all a few years older than me, and I could only imagine the night-mares she must be having.

I met a pretty girl at Theater on the Lake (TOTL) located at Fullerton and the lakefront, after a play that night, Friday, July 15th. Storm clouds were in the air that night, but very little rain. Soft thunder and lightning in the distance, near the Michigan shore, I figured. I could clearly see the light, but the sounds of thunder were only a distant rumble. It was the first time I had ever seen a play there. I had gone because one of my high school pals, Larry, was in the play. The play that night was *Music Man*, a musical, and apparently it was a big deal because it was one of the first plays at TOTL that was di-rected by a woman. Maybe it was the first musical directed by a woman, I can't recall. But it was bright, and all the perform-ers sang so well. Even the young kids were good.

TOTL is not fully enclosed, so you can hear things outside if they are loud enough, and there was no air-conditioning.

Just fans. It was hot and sticky that night, and the performers were sweating bullets on stage. I'll never forget one thing that happened. Just as the two main characters were about to embrace and kiss, the loudest clap of thunder happened just then. It was the only clap of thunder that loud during the show. The entire audience laughed. I enjoyed the play and waited for my buddy outside afterward. When he came out, there was a bunch of people waiting out front of the building. Larry introduced me to the lady who directed the play. I think he said her name was Cindy. She seemed very happy, and thanked me for coming to the show. I recall telling her it was a pleasure to meet her, and asked how she was able to coordinate the thunder at the right moment during the play. She laughed and said, "You're a funny guy, Charlie. Good luck to you." Just then, the main female lead came up behind her, and they hugged. That's when Larry introduced me to her. Her name was Nancy. A very pretty girl, about nineteen, I guessed, from the south side. I was impressed to meet the main character, and I told her she was great. She was friends with Larry, and we immediately smiled at each other, and she seemed so happy. Larry introduced us, as we all went walking through a light drizzle towards the parking lot, under the Lake Shore Drive tunnel. The parking lot was next to the Lincoln Park Zoo. Larry told me to come to the cast party with him. The pretty actress, Nancy, was going too, and she insisted that Larry bring me. Nancy jumped into her mom's car with a couple of people I never met, and I jumped into Larry's car and drove with him to the party not too far away. I'm not sure whose house it was; it was nice and quite a bit like a hippie's, I thought. It didn't matter. I found it interesting with all the candles, incense, and cool furniture. People were happy, and it seemed crowded. People were singing, laughing, drinking, and having a great time. I recall hanging out on the back porch. It was a big first-floor apartment with a big, open back porch looking out to a small lawn and a nice garage. That's where I started talking with Nancy. Nancy was pretty, confident, and sweet. She was the main character in the play, and I asked her if she was a full-time professional actress. She laughed and said, "No, this is a Park District play." I'm not sure if I understood the difference, because it was such a good play. Nancy was so attractive, and still had stage makeup on. Her eyes were dancing blue, and everyone really seemed to love her, especially the kids in the play. She enjoyed laughing, yet she also seemed very smart and wise. I knew she was interested in me that night because she kissed me. It was a quick kiss, and came out of the blue. She said, "I've got to use the ladies' room," and gave me another quick kiss, and said, "Don't go anywhere," and I stayed right there. She came back and said she had called her parents to tell them she was okay and that she would be home soon, but she said her parents had asked her to come home right away because of the Speck murders the night before, and he still had not been caught. I had no idea, but apparently it took place very close to their home on the South Side. She seemed upset, and asked for my number and address. She said she would write me, and gave me her address too. We did write a few times during basic training, but that was the last time I ever saw Nancy. I have always wondered what happened to her.

THE BEATLES WERE performing in Chicago for the second time that summer at the International Amphitheatre, and tickets sold out fast. I was swept up in all the Beatles music, but seeing them wasn't in the cards for me that summer; even though it was on a Thursday, August 11ᵗʰ, and even though I only worked on Saturday and Sunday evenings, I couldn't buy a ticket. The Beatles were so popular, even though John Lennon had said some things about Jesus Christ that didn't seem like a big deal, but he seemed to be explaining what he said every night on the news. Some people seemed so upset about what he had said. I never could understand what the problem was, but they performed to a full house, and all they showed on the news were screaming girls and about three seconds of one song, "Tax Man," which was one of my favorites.

Still, every day throughout that summer, all I could think of was August 18ᵗʰ, because that was the day I had to report for U.S. Navy military service. Every evening at five, Mom would have dinner ready, and I never missed. Mom would become very upset if she made a dinner, and you weren't there to eat it, and didn't let her know well in advance the reason you could not be there. My older brother seemed to have a valid reason for missing most dinners now. He was in college and working all the time, and Mom was proud of him. To me, he was a certifiable genius, and kind of an enigma. Patrick was his name, and hanging out with his younger brother didn't seem the best way for him to enjoy his downtime, which he never seemed to have. Anyway, he was rarely at the table for a meal anymore. He lived at home still, but I rarely saw him. The only valid reason to her, it seemed, was having to work. After dinner, Mom and I would watch Walter

Cronkite's evening news, after watching the local CBS news.

One evening we were watching the news when Cronkite announced that President Johnson was ordering the call-up of an additional 200,000 men for draft because they were needed in Vietnam. Every night there was news of the war, but this announcement hit both me and my mom hard. The war I was hoping to avoid seemed to be getting bigger, and uglier, with Killed in Action (KIA) and wounded American troop counts in the dozens each day. After watching the news that night, we looked at each other, and without saying another word, sadly thought about what might happen to me. I told my mom, before she went to bed, that I was doing everything I could to avoid going over there, and that I thought my chances of serving in the military and avoiding the war were good. She didn't say anything and kissed me good night.

Those were great summer days. Even working at Burger Ville seemed easy and actually interesting. Every Monday morning, I had money for the week. I recall thinking how many days I had left to enjoy the summer before August 18th, and the time seemed to be going by quickly. O August 1, 1966, I woke up thinking, *This is the month*. I had less than three weeks to enjoy each day as much as I could, and then it would be over. I wasn't looking forward to leaving for Orlando, Florida. I was thinking of all those protesters and all those guys supposedly going to Canada to avoid being drafted. I thought about that too. Dad was up there in Canada; perhaps I could go live with him. That notion never seemed to make sense each time I thought about it, so I did my best to make sense out of what I was technically being forced to do. The military always seemed interesting to me, but because of this

Vietnam War that seemed to be getting out of control, I really wanted no part of it. I kept thinking I could get a break with the Navy and pharmacy training and not be called to get involved in Vietnam. I thought for sure I would find a stateside job at some Navy base and get out with benefits so I could go to college. Those college benefits seemed to be the best thing about serving in the U.S. Military, and I would remind myself of those benefits every time I had doubts that summer. I always had doubts and fears, but I figured the die had been cast when I enlisted, so I always reconciled August 18th in my mind. I would survive this, and come back.

I WANTED TO see as many Cubs games as I could. The final game I attended that summer was August 11, 1966, and the Cubs were playing a double header that day. The Houston Astros (formerly Colts) were in town, and this was the final day at home for the Cubs, prior to a long road trip that put them on the road way past August 18th. I saw about a dozen games that summer. Most from bleachers. It didn't matter to me which side I sat on, but this day I started the first game of the double header sitting in the right field bleachers. I had met Richard, the vendor guy, the week before, on a Thursday (Ladies' Day) game against Atlanta. He was older than me, and he was selling "ice-cold Coca-Cola" and made me laugh, because he always said he was so tired. I had seen him around Wrigley before, but on that August 4th game against the Braves, only eleven thousand fans showed up that day, and he had time to chat. He said, "I've been doing this vending for the last three summers, and I attend University of Illinois-Champaign full time during the school year. They haven't called me for the draft because I've got a deferment."

I said, "That's so weird, my brother is on a college deferment too. I got drafted, but I'm going into the Navy this month, on August 18th." He seemed sad to hear that news, but he wished me the best, and said he would find a way to sell his tray of Cokes and come back. I said, "Cool, Richard; nice to meet you finally. I've seen you around here."

Cubs won that day against Atlanta.

The next day the Giants were in town, and they had a great team with Willie Mays, McCovey, Alou, and those great uniforms. I always wanted to watch batting practice from the bleachers because of the show Willie Mays would put on. First he would be shagging flies from teammates hitting in the cage. Just the way he would make that "basket catch" amazed me. When he would eventually get in the batting cage himself, I always hung out in left field, trying to catch (ball hawk) batting practice balls. I caught a few, and even though I had my glove, none of the BP balls came my way that day.

The game from left field that day was fun too. Richard came over and made me laugh with some quip, and believe me, Richard was filled with comebacks and quips. People knew him, and especially the bleacher crowds. Bleacher fans loved him. The regulars anyway. He asked me why I wasn't going to attend college and get a deferment. I explained why I wasn't ready and actually felt some sense of duty. When he heard that, he cringed, shook his head, and walked away calling out, "Ice-cold Coca-Cola! The same Coca-Cola our troops in Vietnam are drinking, folks!" He turned around and mouthed, "I'll see you later." The game ended with a Cubs win that day.

As I was leaving, I looked at the Cubs' upcoming home schedule and saw that they were playing a double header on Thursday, August 11th. That would be my final Cubs game before I left. I was going. I had a few questions for Richard, and heck, it was a double header.

On August 11, I got to Wrigley just before the first pitch, and I was able to walk right up to the ticket window for the bleachers and buy a ticket for a buck, I think. Each day's score-card was fifteen cents. Even though I was at a double header, I only bought one scorecard for the day. I liked to keep my own personal box-score, and I knew all the symbols from Little League and high school baseball. It was fun, because when I attended the games, I couldn't hear Jack Brickhouse and Lloyd Petit call the game. I loved baseball, and this was fun to do.

I did see Richard one last time. He said he had hoped to attend law school after getting his bachelor's degree. He enjoyed the concept of being a lawyer because most of our elected officials were lawyers. To Richard, being a lawyer was the most noble profession, and he felt that being a lawyer al-lowed you so many work options, which meant to him, he would ultimately live a good life, free of financial worries. What Richard was telling me out there in the Wrigley bleach-ers made sense, and I thought that was amazing.

He said, "After you're done with service, I hope you go back to school and perhaps check out law school too. Anyway, think about it," and then he started walking away. "I really hope you survive, Charlie," and he extended his right hand to me for a shake. Then Richard turned around and started with his "ice-cold Coca-Cola" bark. That was the last I ever saw Richard. Anyway, the Cubs split the double header in front of 11,000 fans, and one was me. Somehow, I knew meeting this decent Wrigley Field vendor would always leave a lasting impression upon me. Like being a Cubs fan. If you truly are one, it will leave a very reliable impression upon you.

I recall my final Sunday working at Burger Ville on August 14, 1966. It was hot and muggy, and had rained a little that day. I showed up on time, and my shift partner, Leonard, was busting my chops about this being my final shift before going in. He was funny, but he worked hard, and he always had control of the situation. He taught me everything I needed to know about the job, and he made it easy. We did work hard, and the burgers were flying over the counter. We had dogs, beef sandwiches, fries, onion rings, sodas, and shakes. We always worked it like an assembly line with customers. I don't recall any bad customers at all. Everyone seemed to enjoy the food and simply being at Rush & Oak walking around. When my shift ended, we cleaned up like normal and set everything up for the morning guy, or guys. Leonard would make a call to the boss, and within ten minutes he was walking up to the front door and unlocking it with his keys. That night, he actually smiled at me and said, "Hello, kid." I said, "Hello, boss!" He went directly to the cash register and pulled all the cash out, and a register receipt for his accounting, I guessed. He asked Leonard if everything was done and told us to go home. It was always at 3 a.m., and I was grabbing the El train north as soon as I could. He paid us with cash just before we left, and that night, when he paid me, he wished me good luck and shook my hand. He said, "God bless you," and all I could say was "God bless you too." Just then, he gave me an extra ten bucks and said, "Have a good time before you go in, Charlie," and I never saw him again. He turned out to be a nice man. Really quiet and secretive, but I never felt fear around him, even though we all speculated he was "mobbed up." You never know who you meet sometimes. Anyway, he was a good man to me, and paid me well to do a fun job.

As I was going home that night, I had a weird sensation of how different life was going to become less than a week from quitting Burger Ville. I had no idea what to really expect, but I had made plans for breakfast with my older brother Patrick in less than six hours. I was tired, but my mind was racing. I needed at least a couple hours of sleep after my thirty-minute ride back home.

EIGHT A.M., AUGUST 15, 1966 came quickly. I had agreed to meet with my older brother, and I was really looking forward to this. He had a regular summer job near Irving Park Road and Broadway, so we had agreed to meet at The Alps, which was on the corner there, at nine. He said the meal would be on him, and he wanted to talk. I showered off all the food smell funk from the night before and made it to The Alps about 8:50. I always seemed to be early. My brother showed up exactly at nine, which was typical of him. We met outside the front door, and he said, "So, you hungry?" I said, "Sure." We went in, and the hostess sat us in a booth facing Irving Park Road. We ordered coffee and juice, and looked at the menu.

He said, "It's good to see you again," and asked how I was feeling.

I said, "Fine," and then I told him that I quit my job last night because of that-coming Thursday. I told him it was a cool job and it paid well. He said he had heard all about it. The amazing thing about my older brother was he seemed to somehow know everything I was doing. I figured it was Mom, but sometimes I wondered how he got his intel on me. It seemed uncanny how much he knew.

The waitress came back with juice, and poured our coffee into the upside-down mugs sitting on the table. Patrick ordered pancakes and sausage, and I ordered two eggs, over easy, with potatoes and toast. Patrick told me he was returning to college full time in two weeks, and that his summer job would turn into a part-time job so he could pay tuition and rent. I decided to do as much listening as I could during this final breakfast together. The waitress returned so fast with our food, we were actually startled. Patrick said, "Looks good," and we both gobbled what was on our plates quietly. That was how my family always ate. As soon as food was served, we became quiet, so this pause in our conversation wasn't anything new to either one of us. When we finished our meals, we talked for a short time, and he asked for the check and said he had to get back to work. I asked him if he would write to me, but not actually write. I said, "Can you send me the Cubs box scores from the *Tribune* from time to time?" I didn't want him to feel obligated to write, but I told him receiving box scores in the mail from time to time would be important for me. He said he would keep that in mind, and he would do his best. He said his boss had given him an early lunch for us to spend some time together. As we got up from our booth, I thanked him for the meal, and for sending box scores when he could, and he said, "No problem, it was my pleasure, and I'll do what I can with box scores." We walked outside to the corner of Broadway and Irving Park Road and then he said something that has stayed with me every day since that moment.

"What you're about to do will not be easy, Charlie. When they call for volunteers at any time during your military service, don't be compelled to step forward. I know you, Charlie; not stepping forward to participate is not who you are, but I'm telling you to think about what I am telling you, because I want you to survive this."

I listened intently to every word, and he said it in a way I don't think I'd ever heard him say anything. I had been thinking this same thing about surviving this since my eighteenth birthday. I responded, "Yeah, I figured that out, and I'm doing everything I can within the rules to avoid Vietnam."

He said, "Good, I hope you do avoid it. Maybe you'll be assigned to some place in Europe. Take care, and write home," he said and shook my hand in a different way, and before he turned around, he said, "Just do your best, Charlie." It seemed more sincere for some reason. He said, "I've got to get back," and turned around and started jogging back towards his job only a few blocks away.

I didn't have any plans that day, but I knew I was sad for some reason. I decided to go to the lakefront by Waveland, and as soon as I got near the tennis courts, I sat down and cried for some reason. I know I wasn't sure why I was sad and crying these massive tears that were dripping on the concrete in front of this bench. I just knew I was actually weeping privately more than I had ever wept before. I think I sat at that bench near the tennis courts for an hour before gathering myself and walking slowly toward The Rocks along the lake that day. I ended up spending the entire day there, swimming, walking, and swimming all along the way towards Montrose Harbor. It was a very hot and humid day, and the lake water was a refreshing sixty-eight (f) degrees. That was a wonderful day that I will always remember.

I don't recall that Tuesday or Wednesday much. I remember having dinner at home with my mom quietly on the Wednesday before August 18, 1966. After dinner, we watched the news, and Cronkite mentioned President Johnson calling up more troops for service in Vietnam. We both looked at each other, yet said nothing. We knew this wasn't good news, but I tried to reassure her that my chances of not going to Vietnam were good. She listened, but I knew she simply wasn't as confident about my military prospects as I was. She seemed far more worried about this than I was, even though I know I was really worried. I tried to keep her calm. We reminded each other of the early wake-up for me the next day. She said she would get up at 4:30 to get me up and make me a good breakfast. I said, "Okay, as long as I'm out at the front door before 6:00 a.m. when the ride gets here, I'm looking forward to it." I fell asleep quickly, and before I knew it, Mom was knocking on the door and said, "It's time to get up. I will make bacon and eggs with toast."

I said, "Okay, thank you," and headed toward the bathroom and took a shower. I got dressed and packed a toothbrush and toothpaste, and made sure I had all my identification and paperwork I had already signed a couple months ago. I was told that was all I would need when I got picked up.

Mom's timing with breakfast that morning was perfect. Everything was warm, and the eggs were perfect. After I ate, I said, "I should go out there and wait for the ride now."

She gave me a hug and said, "Make sure you write, and be safe."

"I'll write at least once a week, and Patrick said he would send Cubs box scores."

She nodded, we hugged and kissed, and I went to wait outside for the ride downtown. It only took about ten minutes and this Navy guy drove up in a nice-looking gray sedan. I got in the front seat. He said, "We have a few stops to make along the way." I was his first pickup.

I said, "Thank you," and realized there was no turning back now. I also hoped I wouldn't get carsick, because this guy was driving crazy.

WE ARRIVED AT an old building that seemed to have been used for decades. Dark, with shiny marble and cold cement floors. There was a waiting room where we were told to relax, and they would call us. After an hour, an Army guy came into the front of the room with manila packets and called out everyone in the room. He said, "Is there anyone I have not called?" One guy said, "Me," and the soldier called him up to the front to ask his name. He instructed the guy to sit tight, and he would resolve the situation. I thought that guy seemed intense, but really neat, with really shiny shoes. He was older than me, but at this point, everyone seemed older than me. We were instructed NOT to open our folders and stay seated. He also mentioned where the latrine was located. That was good, because I had to go. I got back to my seat and just sat there with my packet on my lap. It was sealed and had my last name and the last four digits of my social security number on it.

Another hour passed, and another Army soldier came into the room. He said, "I need you to line up and get ready for your cursory physical. We will march single file into the corridor, and follow me to the doctor's inspection room. Is this understood?" We all said, "Yes sir," and he seemed disgusted but said, "Okay, follow me."

We walked single file in this long, dark, and cold corridor, finally turning in to another big room with long yellow lines on both sides. At that point, I realized there were about twenty of us being inducted, or enlisting, like me. I do recall the moment the first of three doctors in long white coats said, "Please remove all your clothes at this time." Wow! This seemed sudden, I thought. Everyone immediately started to remove their clothes quickly. I joined in, and thought, *This already sucks.* Just get it done, I figured. I realized at that moment, privacy was no longer to be expected, and I removed all my clothes.

One doctor checked the heart, mouth, neck, scalp, and ears, while another checked hands, toes, legs, and back. The final doctor was the one I had heard about, but forgot to expect, because everything was moving so fast. He stepped up to each guy and asked them to turn around and spread their butt cheeks. I realized sometime after that, he was checking to make sure we had all our junk, and didn't have hemorrhoids. Not a horrible experience, but I had never done this with a room full of dudes. I guess I passed. We were told to put our clothes back on and go wait in the waiting room to be called. The soldier who led us in took us back.

The rest of the day was paperwork at school-type desks. There were tons of forms to complete, and each box had to be filled out a very precise way according to the soldier instructing us. He told us three times before we started NOT to get ahead of him. Nobody did, because he seemed extremely serious when he said, "Don't fucking get ahead of me!" I was told I was going to get on a train the next day at 0600 with eight other guys heading toward Orlando. They had arranged a decent hotel room at the south end of Michigan Avenue loop for the night. One guy was given everything for all of us, which included our packets, tickets, and some cash. Why he was chosen, I don't know, but as long as he didn't hassle me, I was fine with that. We were put on a small bus and driven to our hotel for the night. I remember wanting to call one of my friends but needed to relax, so I took a walk in Grant Park. I walked around the Buckingham Fountain and saw the lights for the first time. I had seen the fountain before, but never at night. I sat down at a bench and watched it for hours, until it was completely dark. I was hungry, and I reminded myself that our dinner would be paid for in advance. All I had to do was go to the hotel restaurant and give my name. The walk back to the hotel only took five minutes, and the food was terrific. I went right to my room and lay down.

AT 4:30 A.M., I woke up to a loud pounding on my door. "Kinane, we got to meet downstairs in fifteen minutes," a voice yelled. I jumped up in a daze, opened the door a crack, and said, "Okay, I'll be there." I took a quick shower, brushed my teeth, and put on the clothes I was wearing the day before. I smelled them first, and they didn't seem to stink, and I had no other choice. I got down to the lobby, and I was the last guy they were waiting for. The guy with all our records said, "We're going to walk down to the induction center because it's only four blocks." We all agreed and followed the guy. Quick walk back.

As soon as we got there, we were lined up again and put on a bus to Union Station for our train ride to Orlando, Florida. The bus ride was quick, and we got to the station just on time. The conductor seemed very serious as he looked at his pocket watch and said, "We held the train for you boys an extra five minutes; show me your tickets please." We all got on, and the train started moving. The conductor showed us the train car restaurant and then to our Pullman car. We each had our own rooms. I entered mine, and thought this was so nice. It had a bed that folded out and a tiny bathroom. I can't remember if it had a shower, but it definitely had a sink and toilet. I sat down, and for the next thirty-two long hours, I rode that train, ate good food, and stopped at stations along the way south I can't even remember now. I do recall some-one saying, "We're in Georgia." He said that because of the overwhelming humidity. I had never felt that type of humid-ity, and one of the guys said, "It's even more humid where we're going." I was just trying to absorb everything and not talk too much. I wanted to listen, and these guys could talk. They joked and laughed with each other, and I tried to seem interested in what they were saying, but all I could think of was basic training, and what the heck that was going to be like.

WHEN THE TRAIN finally arrived in Orlando, it was hot and humid and late at night. The guy with all the records made a call as directed from a phone booth. We waited only ten or fifteen minutes before another small bus arrived to pick us up. The driver was a large, squared-away sailor of about twenty-three, I'd guess. He was older than me for sure. He was given our records, and told us, "Say 'Here!' when you hear your name. When you say 'here,' move to the door of the bus." He called my name first. "Kinane, Charles Kinane." I moved quickly to the door of the bus, and he asked me in a quiet voice what my social security number was. I gave him my number as he confirmed it on my packet. He said, "Fill in the seats from the back of the bus first, after I tell you to enter the bus." I was quite tired and groggy, but I stepped onto the bus as quickly as I could and found a seat in the back of the bus. I heard him call out the other guys' names, and they entered the bus. As we all settled into our seats, he said, "Stay quiet please. I will be taking you to Naval Training Center, Orlando. When we arrive I will take you to the recruit in-processing facility, but we call it RIFF, so while you are in this facility before being assigned your training unit, you will be known as RIFF. Is that understood?"

We all said, "Yes, sir."

He exploded and said, "I am Petty Officer Wonder; I work for a living! And only call officers sir, and ONLY salute officers and the flag. Is that clear?"

We all said, "Yes, Petty Officer Wonder!"

He sat down and took us to the NTC, Orlando. I might as well have been on the moon. I knew things were going to be totally different now. This wasn't a game, and I wanted to listen to everything, do exactly as I was told, and stay out of trouble. *I'll survive this*, I thought.

THE THING I remember about being a RIFF was the fact that I wanted my hair cut. I saw clearly that the next simple step in this process was not sticking out, and believe me, RIFF stuck out. We were heckled as we marched to mess hall for meals for two days. I didn't have really long hair, but I needed a haircut three weeks ago. I wanted to blend in, and as soon as I could get my haircut done, blending in would be easier and less verbally abusive. It felt so good to get that done, as I recall. I felt like I was actually getting on the team. We already were issued our clothes for basic training, so right after getting our hair cut, we were broken up into two "beta" training units. Turns out, this NTC wasn't officially opening until July 1967. As with everything the military does, it must be tested. This was the first and only NTC of the big three (Great Lakes, San Diego, and now Orlando in 1967) to anticipate the need for basic training for women. Males and females rarely interacted, except during "workweek" if they were assigned work in the galley/mess hall," which was a VERY hard workweek assignment I was lucky to avoid. I had a job as runner for "Brig" building. I think this was a reward for my running ability. I was assigned with another recruit, a black guy about my age, and we got along fine. We both understood what this was all about and stayed inside our little office, waiting for someone to give us a command, like sweep this hallway, or police the outside of the building, and empty trash cans. Compared to our fellow training unit mates working in the mess hall or galley, we had it so easy. That lasted a week.

We were assigned our training unit, which was about seventy guys as I recall. We were going to be together, sharing everything for the next eight weeks. We were marched to our building and assigned a rack. We were assigned a footlocker. We were told where the "head" was located. As soon as we all had our racks assigned, we heard, "Attention on deck! ATTENTION ON DECK! Line up in front of your footlockers on the black line! Now, double time, double time!" Some guys stumbled around, but everyone seemed to figure out what to do fast.

I glanced over, and the sailor barking out these orders was young; wearing all white, with a yellow rope around one of his arms. He explained who he was; the yellow cord represented that he was assistant company commander (ACC) for this training unit. He definitely had a southern sound and seemed angry all the time. He explained all the basics. The dos and don'ts of Navy basic training. He said, "Think of this facility as your ship. Front is bow at that door; the bow is Company Commander Petty Officer Gibbons' office, and he will be here soon. So, front," pointing to the door to my right, "bow," he pointed at the opposite side of the room towards the offices, "and head. Right: starboard side; left port side." I realized I had to start thinking and absorbing quickly here. Everything he said, he asked, "Is that clear?" He expected a very loud "Aye! Aye!" We all responded with a robust "Aye, Aye!" We did so from that moment on for the next eight weeks.

After about ten minutes, Company Commander Gibbons walked in. He was a short man, but he looked experienced, and he was a petty officer first class, which seemed incredible to me at the time. He was salty and direct. He walked down each side of the training unit and introduced himself to us, while we were at attention again in front of our footlockers. He was about five-foot-six, but there was no chance any one of us would ever challenge him physically. First of all, he seemed fair, but serious. He said, "The most important thing for the next eight weeks is for you to listen to commands and respond as a training unit. This is a test training unit, and you will make my Navy proud, is that understood? You will be challenged. You will obey direct orders. You will finish basic training and make my Navy proud. If you do not respond to training, we will find a way to try to motivate you to respond to Navy training. That means cycling, that means intensive training if cycling doesn't help, and finally motivational training, in the event intensive training doesn't help, and not one of you swinging dicks in the training unit want that level of training, because it's not optional. It's only for dumbasses, and I won't tolerate any dumbasses in my training unit. Is that understood?"

"Aye! Aye!" we screamed.

He told us to get our bunks and footlockers squared away, and be "At ease." He said he'd be back soon, and left with the ACC. From that moment on, we were addressed as "Recruit" individually, or "Swinging Dicks," as a unit. Seemed funny, but all I wanted to do was get through this and not raise my profile, by keeping quiet, and listening. That seemed to be the key to all this.

Every day was the same basic routine. Wake up early, shit, shower, shave (SSS), make your rack, dress, and be ready to stand at attention a lot. March as a unit a lot. Sit in classes learning Uniform Code of Military Justice (UCMJ), fire prevention, and most importantly, our eleven General Orders. We were expected to give the correct General Order at any time we were asked. I tried to memorize all of them verbatim, but prayed never to be called on one of the eleven I might not recall upon command.

Basic training was exhausting, but I was able to gain some positive recognition for my running ability. Every other day, we would run three miles. The other days were for calisthenics. Running came easy, because of my running days in high school. I seemed to have no problem always being the first guy to finish. Some days even running in BoonDocker training boots and long pants. The CC never said anything, but

I could sense from the way he watched, he seemed to take pride in my running on behalf of his unit each time I finished.

In addition to day-to-day "unit cycling" sessions for having a few beds not made correctly or something about the head not being perfectly cleaned each day, it was always something. It was the CC's way of getting us in great physical shape, while expecting full compliance with his orders. He never let up on us either. He explained why he would "cycle" us, so it made sense for some reason. "Cycling" is a spontaneous way to correctly motivate you, or the entire unit, when commands weren't obeyed, or some seemingly minor failure to succeed happened. It happened multiple times a day, and we would be cycled, inside or outside. If for some reason, the CC thought you did something a little more egregious, he sent you to his boss, Chief Petty Officer Drewash. The ACC and CC had been making threats of intensive training (IT) and motivational training (MT or MOTOUR), but only Chief Drewash could make that judgment, and Chief Drewash didn't like anybody. I was sentenced to IT four times at NTC Orlando. I met Chief Drewash four times. Never pleasant, but the first time, he scared the crap out of me because I didn't enter his office properly. He jumped up and screamed, "STOW THAT BALL CAP, RECRUIT! STOW THAT BALL CAP!"

I had forgotten to stow the ball cap in my belt as instructed, and walked in his office holding it in my left hand. I turned directly to him and said, "Permission to try again, Chief?"

He screamed, "DO IT, AND ENTER IN THE PROPER WAY!"

I immediately left his office, and he sat down. I knocked again three times and almost forgot to put the ball cap in my belt again, but as he said, "Enter" in the most stressed way I have ever heard, I entered and sounded off properly. He sentenced me to IT and dismissed me.

IT was that night after evening chow. Those sentenced that day met in an air-conditioned hangar that had a stage. There were about twenty of us lined up as directed facing the stage. We were at ease, but silent. Several ACC guys I didn't know were there to watch us. A man in uniform walked up to the mic on stage and said, "I'm Senior Chief Parker. I'm not here to help you lose weight or get you more prepared for your PT test. I'm here to punish you. You will do several exercises over the next hour, and you must do them correctly, or one of the ACCs walking around monitoring you will give you a mark for not doing these exercises correctly."

I remember not turning my head, but using my peripheral vision to look at everyone around me. Everyone seemed scared to death, and frankly I was too. The first time was weird.

He continued, "If you receive three marks from any of the ACCs monitoring you, you will return tomorrow night, and the next night, until you no longer make three mistakes in one night. IS THAT CLEAR?!?

We all shouted, "Yes, Senior Chief!"

I ended up sentenced four times for the most minor, ridiculous things, but I certainly recall the fourth time I was at IT was very easy. I was getting in the best shape of my life. We had been trained in fire prevention and weapons (M-16 and .45-caliber handgun), and tested on swimming. We were also trained on how to function on board a ship during basic training. My goal of keeping a low profile didn't help as much as I thought. In addition to daily cycling with the training unit, I spent some time at IT, but never MT, thank goodness.

Now, I got to understand MT up close during my work-week at basic training. MT was done in a room inside the brig building. Three hours of far more difficult exercises, but all done while holding a fourteen-pound M-4 (WWII) rifle without any rounds. One offender and six regular sailors, including a corpsman. I saw three recruits heading to this disciplinary procedure, which was a last-ditch effort to motivate a recruit before he is actually being sentenced to time in the brig. All three I saw pass me in the hallway ended up in tears within an hour. I recall understanding that MT was a very subtle form of torture in my mind. Ugly stuff, and I'm so glad I never experienced MT myself. Another reason to stay low profile and do what you're told to do.

As those eight weeks wrapped up and we finally went through Pass-In-Review, the CC finally brought us into his office, one by one. He was giving us our next assignment, which meant for most of us A-School. When he called my name, I entered his office as trained. He told me I was going to Hospital Corpsman School, San Diego, and then said, "So, you want to be a pecker checker, eh? You want to be a shankar mechanic. Eh? Well, good luck to you, Kinane. You've done very well here at NTC Orlando, in my training unit, and I wish you good luck." He looked at my packet one more time for about a minute, and I just stood there in silence. He said, "You're a good man, Kinane. You've impressed a lot of people here. You're in great physical shape, and you run faster and longer than a lot of the staff have ever seen. Think about UDT-SEALs. Dismissed."

I turned sharply around and left his office, thinking *Thank God, I got my A-School*, but he said nothing about my C-School request of pharmacy tech training. *UDT-SEALs*, I thought. *What is that?*

I soon found out.

The night of our Pass-in-Review was my first liberty off base. I had a few bucks in my pocket, and tagged along with a few of the guys in the training unit. I ended up at a local strip joint called Port Liberty and was amazed at how many sailors were there, all in uniform like me. Furthermore, I was totally amazed at how beautiful all these naked women looked. I was eighteen and having a difficult time hiding my "chub" while finding a seat with a table along one of the walls. I could see everything, and I'm sure my mouth was completely wide open for at least five minutes looking at all the amazing naked women running all around that big room. I think I laughed at myself when I actually caught myself about to drool. I didn't but almost. I was still eighteen, but Florida beer rules, even off base, were okay for eighteen. I ordered a Chicago Old Style beer, like most of the other guys, and it tasted so good. After I took my second gulp of that bottle, the most beautiful blonde lady walked up in front of me and asked me for a dance. I had no idea what that really meant, but as I tried to stand up, she said, "It's five dollars, and I'm the only one who dances, and you can't touch me. Okay, honey?"

With my mouth laying on the table and my eyes staring at her amazing body and skin, I said, "Sure." I dug in my pocket for my bills and gave her five bucks. Her dance right in front of me, and sometimes rubbing parts of her body on me, was so incredible. I'm not sure what happened the rest of that night, but I did make it back to the base and training unit before curfew. I took a cab, and I recall being so excited about the strip joint and the beautiful blonde that I had an erection that wouldn't go away. I was very aware that it was creating an obvious bulge in my white pants. I got out of the cab, showed the guy at the gate my ID, trying to stay turned away from him the entire time. I walked about three hundred yards to the building where my unit slept. I walked in the bow door and quickly walked to the recruit sergeant at arms, who was this very large Mexican guy of about twenty-three. A nice guy, and he didn't have liberty that night. I said, "Do you mind if I take a shower?"

He said, "No, but make sure you wipe everything down, because we have inspection tomorrow morning."

I said thank you and headed straight to the head.

He said, "You should make that a cold shower, Kinane," and laughed.

I said, "Roger that," and took a nice cold shower. It seemed to help as I recall.

I've never forgotten that first liberty. Two days later, I was on a plane headed toward San Diego, California, for Navy Hospital Corpsman A-School. I had never been to California, and couldn't wait to get there. I declined two weeks' leave back home because I wanted to see California so much. It was the middle of October 1966.

Corpsman School:

THE ONLY THING I recall about Hospital Corpsman School (A-School) at Naval Regional Medical Center (NRMC), Balboa, located in San Diego, California, is this. I remember morning muster, looking east towards the sunset coming up from behind the mountains to the east. I thought it was glorious. I also recall my main teacher, Lt. Aggie. She was short with dark hair and narrow facial features. She was also a registered nurse, and she took this training very seriously. She was an attractive woman, but far more, a person of great respect and dignity. She was married and lived off base. She really cared about our training, and took time to get to know all twenty of us in the class. It lasted ten weeks and concluded late January 1967. I learned a lot there, and stood regular duty. I basically learned everything an emergency medical technician (EMT) would learn, and then some. I know I paid close attention every day and tried not to stick out, but embrace this training, in the hope that good grades overall would tilt the C-School chances in my favor.

Downtown San Diego was quite run down at that time, and only a mile or two away from the NRMC. I rarely ventured off base, but when I did, I walked downtown to check it out. It was a sailors' port town, that's for sure. Grimy, I thought. I also ventured to Balboa Park across from NRMC, and one time to the zoo. On my final weekend of A-School, I tagged along with a couple of guys in my class on a Saturday morning. We headed down to Mission Beach. I had never been in the Pacific Ocean, and today was the day. I enjoyed that day at the beach very much.

Two days before graduation that final week of January 1967, we had our meetings individually with Lt. Aggie. She was so very pleasant. As I sat across from her at her desk, I was thinking *This is a serious and very dignified woman.* I wasn't sure how old she was, but I thought maybe thirty. She was probably closer to twenty-five, but I'm bad at guessing ages. I couldn't help but notice she was very attractive and appeared to have a smoking hot body. I imagined that in the split second it takes to imagine anything while she was reading reports, grades, summaries, and giving her personal summary. She pointed out far more positives, and suggested more work on other topics. She was interesting, I thought, genuine, and I really appreciated that at that time. She had good leadership skills. She congratulated me on finishing Hospital Corpsman School and explained the graduation process and departure from NRMC. She also told me that I would be getting my pharmacy tech C-School at NRMC Portsmouth, Virginia, but only after completing Marine Field Medical Service School (FMSS) at Camp Pendleton. I would go straight from NRMC San Diego to Camp Pendleton four hours after graduation. I would go by bus, because every one of my classmates was going straight to FMS training too. "We serve Marines in the field, Charlie. You agreed to this job, and you'll be fine at FMS training. It only lasts five weeks." Then Lt. Aggie said words that haunt me still. "We're at war, Charlie, and U.S. Marines need us too."

I said, "Yes, Lieutenant," and thanked her before I left her office.

While the next classmate went in, I just stood there, outside her office door, thinking about this wrinkle in my plans. Somehow, and I'm not sure why, but I didn't expect FMSS. I thought I would go straight to pharmacy C-School. I shook my head and thought to myself, *Stay focused. You'll get through this. You'll survive this.*

I don't recall the graduation at all, but I do recall the next five and a half weeks at Camp Pendleton.

I ARRIVED AT Camp Pendleton within an hour of my A-School graduation from Navy Hospital Corpsman School. I didn't expect this, but a little different. I had gotten my third strip, which meant I was now an E-3, like a corporal to Marines. As soon as I got off the bus, I realized I was being treated different, and with far more respect. The United States Marine Corp (USMC) likes corpsmen. Corpsmen are "Doc," and quite possibly the last line of defense in terms of life and death on any battlefield. Corpsmen have been crucial every time Marines engage. Marines respect corpsmen, as long as they are respectful too. Corpsmen will rarely be accepted as real Marines, but they are crucial as "Doc." Especially on battlefields for generations. *It is a good feeling,* I thought, *and after five weeks, I'm off to Portsmouth, Virginia. I can handle this. Bring on FMS.*

I had no idea how much I would eat those words.

We were assigned a group of ten Navy corpsmen for the five weeks of training—basically, all the guys from my

A-School, with only a few exceptions—and I wasn't concerned about those things. I was concerned about surviving, and dealing with this unexpected challenge.

USMC GUNNY SERGEANT Bielow was assigned to my class. He was in his thirties, I had guessed, and spoke with a slight British accent. He mentioned right away that he was born in England and moved to the U.S. when he was a young teenager. He was about five-foot, eight-inches tall and in great shape. He'd served in Vietnam already and even served during the Korean War. His father was killed fighting Nazis in France, and he and his mom moved to Dartmouth, Massachusetts. He said he had lived there since moving to the States, and his wife and mom were there. He was hard-core serious every day he was training. He demanded we all understood and experienced handling trauma as much as he wanted us to learn. He focused on what we would definitely experience and in particular what we would experience in the war zone. He made sure we turned off any Hollywood movie type of thinking.

"The real war zone is uglier. The war zone is a toxic environment where troops are exposed to shit that might shock you when you see it. The war zone is not all bullets and bombs. The war zone is broken bones, bruises, sprained ankles, twisted necks, broken fingers, temporary blindness, concussions, battle fatigue, shell shock, and mental illness." He said this, and more, every day of FMS training. "The war zone IS bullets, and bombs too. The war zone is pain management and triage." He was a true leader, and spoke with genuine passion about our jobs, but he also had a pleasant side when he wasn't working. When he felt at ease, he was funny and engaging. He enjoyed technology and science. He recognized that this would not be like basic training at all, and that our skills would be needed by USMC all over the world.

He said, "You're important to Marines, men. I'm going to do my best to give you all the skills you need in the field when a Marine needs your help. Call me Gunny, just Gunny. I will call you Doc, and every Marine you meet here will call you that too." He continued to give us the five-week program, which was mostly inside class work, but he emphasized the one week of field training. "Don't expect that to be easy. Is that clear?

We all responded, "Yes, Gunny."

I thought to myself, *I don't like getting dirty. Okay, bring it on.* We were dismissed for the remainder of the day and expected to muster at 0700 in our navy dungarees the next morning. Basically after morning chow.

We all mustered in front of the training building the next morning. Gunny Bielow was already there and answering questions. I noticed he had a full chest of medals, including a Purple Heart, so that alone told me he had seen combat. I was immediately impressed with him, and I was curious about his background, so I asked him if he was born in London. He said, "No, Burnley, Lancashire."

I asked, "Is that near London?"

He just looked at me and didn't answer, but he said, "We'll

talk more when time permits." He did mention he played guitar and performed off base at a local club from time to time.
"Perhaps we can meet there some evening, with the rest of
your class," he said. I thought, *Hey, sure. That sounded cool.*
He said, "Nice meeting you, Kinane. Where are you from?"
I said, "Chicago," and he said, "Cold up there, eh? Let's get
going." He asked us all to line up and respond "Here" when
we heard our name called. We all responded, and he walked
us into the building.

The class was small and had regular classroom desks.
Gunny Bielow explained the entire course — who, what,
where — and instructed us to line up and walk to another
room where we were issued our green uniforms. Two of each:
pants, shirts, hats, socks. We were instructed to use our basic
training-issued BoonDocker boots. We were to start every day
by mustering at 0700, Monday through Friday, for class. The
final week would be in the field, and we would all be together
roughing it for the final week. He said, "Everything leads up
to that final week, so be prepared. Thousands of Navy corpsmen have come through this training, and I am confident you
will be fine." Each day, after class work, we were released
around 1600, and the evenings were ours for liberty.

Liberty for me was almost entirely on base. I wasn't comfortable off base. I really never was comfortable off most
of the bases I served on. There was so much to do on base.
Bowling, library, basketball, twelve-inch softball, which was
new to me being from Chicago, where sixteen-inch was the
rage. I wasn't comfortable leaving base, and I always figured
there was plenty to do on base, including studying and reading letters and box scores I received. Writing back. Keeping a

low profile and doing my best while here was my goal here at A-School. I wanted to leave good impressions. I wanted to learn, and I wanted to feel squared away. I didn't want to spend too much money, because I didn't have a lot. The only time I took my liberty off base was the one night, about week three, when Gunny Bielow said he would be playing his guitar at this local pub just outside the front gate called Whiskey Jar, which wanted to let Camp Pendleton know this was a USMC-friendly place. Jarheads and their paychecks were very welcome, and on or near the first and fifteenth of every month, the cash was flowing at Whiskey Jar, and so were a few fights. They were still cool enough to offer open stage on certain Friday evenings. A show. All you had to do was sign up. However, there was no question, this was definitely a Marine bar.

It was an average-sized bar, with tables near the stage, a well-stocked bar with nice stools. Clean and organized. One black-and-white TV near the ceiling in the corner above the head was showing a Dodgers game without the sound. I ordered a cold Schlitz on draft, with a burger and fries from the bar. I think I paid two bucks for the entire meal, He said they'd bring it out to me, so I sat down at a table by myself. Just as my burger and beer came to me, five guys from my FMS class came in laughing and talking loud. They saw me and said, "Hey, Kinane," and grabbed stools at the bar.

Gunny Bielow was introduced just as I started attacking my burger and fries. The cold mug of Schlitz was perfect. Gunny walked on stage to quiet applause, sat down, and started playing the most amazing guitar solo. I wasn't sure what kind of music it was, but he seemed to have an amazing grasp on everything. His skills were so impressive, which included a way of hitting the notes on the frets I had never seen. I have always enjoyed live music when it's good. I will always recall how talented Gunny Bielow was on that guitar. He didn't sing, but he played three numbers on the guitar. I was really impressed because his playing on that acoustic guitar seemed so perfect. Almost effortless. I'm not sure why he didn't sing, but I know I was impressed, and applauded with enthusiasm. While clapping, I looked at the guys from my class at the bar, and they were all looking at me, and I could tell they were thinking, *Suck-up*, but I was truly impressed with Gunny's performance. The only guitarist I could recall with those type of skills on guitar was Django Reinhardt, and I told Gunny I thought he actually might be better than Django. He knew exactly who I was talking about and simply said, "Thank you, Kinane." That was the only time I heard him perform, and I told him he was awesome as he came off the stage, walking towards the end of the bar. He said a very gracious "Thank you!" That was also the only time I saw him in civilian clothes (civvies).

Shortly after Gunny finished, I left the pub so I could get back to the base before 9 p.m. I just wasn't comfortable off base at that time, and I was trying to keep everything simple.

The day before our field week, we were issued helmets, unloaded M-16, and other corpsman gear, and told to muster outside as normal at 0500 the next morning. The week was difficult, but weather was reasonable and not too hot, so each day went by quickly. We trained on triage and how to manage wounds. We slept on the ground and ate C-rations all week. I actually lost ten pounds that week because C-rations are difficult to open, heat up, and not really tasty at all. The one thing I did learn is when you're really hungry, any food tastes good, and is happily eaten. I can tell you that when we made it back to the training building to turn in gear temporarily issued for that week, we were dismissed. The shower that evening lasted longer than regular military showers. I just don't recall ever being that dirty. Dirt was everywhere on my body and seemingly in every crevice.

After the show, I watched some TV in the common room and hit my rack early. I was exhausted. When field week was over, I knew the next day was our final day of FMS training, and that was the day we would receive our next orders. I started praying I wouldn't have to be in the field, getting filthy again. I was hoping I would be heading straight to Portsmouth, Virginia, and avoid Vietnam.

The next day, we mustered one final time outside the training building, and as soon as we sat down at the desks we had occupied for the last four weeks, Gunny Bielow called out names. He wanted each person to come up to him when called. He wanted to congratulate us individually, give us a certificate for finishing FMS training, and tell us quietly where we were going next. After receiving their orders quietly from Gunny, the others were all dismissed and left the room. Gunny called me last for some reason, but everyone he had called up before me looked concerned because they were headed directly to Vietnam with the U.S. Marines 3rd Infantry division. When he called me up, he stared at me as I approached him. He told me, "Congratulations, Kinane, you did well here at FMS training," and gave me the certificate.

He leaned into me and said, "How did you get so lucky not to go directly to Vietnam to serve my Marines? You're headed directly to pharmacy C-School, Portsmouth, Virginia. I'm happy for you, Kinane. Keep up the great work, and maybe you'll be lucky to serve Marines in the field someday. We're not too different, Kinane." He continued by telling me that he enlisted as a Navy corpsman, but when he had the chance to shift over to USMC, he did, because it was a bigger challenge. He said, "You have amazing stamina, strength, and skills, Kinane. You should consider USMC and switch, or maybe even UDT-SEAL team. You're good, sailor."

I remember looking him in the eyes for about ten seconds, nodding my head, and saying, "Yes, Gunny. Thank you, Gunny," and I turned around, trying to hide my enormous happy moment by getting C-School. Gunny had also given me my airline ticket for the next day. I couldn't think of anything else for the entire evening, and thought to myself, *You lucky stiff. You lucky stiff. Maybe I'll be fine and avoid serving in the Vietnam war zone.* I was thrilled, and thought all my hopes and prayers were panning out. After we were dismissed and instructed where to be the next morning, we went back to our four-man rooms to clear out our lockers, do laundry, and put everything neatly folded in our duffle bags. I recall thinking my duffle bag was overfilled now because of the new green uniform issued clothing. It didn't seem to matter, because I was still giddy with the news of C-School next. I figured, *I'm going to survive this and enjoy my service going forward.* I felt really lucky compared to my fellow classmates. They were all quiet that night and didn't say much. A few guys asked me how I got C-School so fast. I told them I had requested it with my recruiter, and it seems he really came through with his recommendation. I was conflicted about my good fortune, but focused on being ready for the first bus to the airport the next morning. I was leaving Pendleton, and headed to the East Coast.

Pharmacy C-School:

I DON'T REMEMBER the flight from San Diego, California, to Norfolk, Virginia. I don't recall the shuttle ride from Norfolk airport to Portsmouth Naval Medical Center (PNMC). I don't remember checking into the school. I was living in a building that doubled as a classroom building and dorm facility all in one. I had a small dorm room that I shared with another classmate. I don't recall his name, because we both kept to ourselves, and he had different interests than I did, but we got along as dorm mates. Not buddies. I remember his face and not his name.

Portsmouth Navy Pharmacy Tech C-School was scheduled to last six months, and we started classes on February 12, 1967. We had classes Monday through Friday, from about 8 a.m. to 5 p.m., which always gave us time for morning chow at the hospital cafeteria. We all were assigned extra duty in the actual pharmacy at PNMC about once a week. Class focus was on anatomy and physiology, chemistry and chemicals, math, which focused on ratios and proportion, Latin abbreviation, and medical terms. After the first few weeks, we expanded to compounding. Each and every day including typing on old manual typewriters. We were continuously being tested, and soon we could type fifteen prescription labels in under twenty minutes, by reading dummy prescriptions. I recall that to truly be a challenge, but I did have a high school typing class that helped. I was able to satisfy this requirement way before the final week. Classes were intense, and all taught by first class or second class petty officers. All the teachers were men. Of the thirty people in the class, two were women.

Outside of class, during our liberty time, I typically found things on base to do, like twelve-inch softball, tennis, bowling, and right next to the dorm class building was the NCO club, so going off base didn't appeal to me, until that summer.

I recall one of my classmate buddies, Mike from Taos, New Mexico, talking me into going to Virginia Beach during that summer of 1967 with him and a couple other guys in his car. Mike was a great guy with a great sense of humor. He was able to turn his serious on and off easily. Most of all, he was a decent guy. He spoke like a surfer to me. His car was a very cool 1964 Plymouth Belvedere. Very slick, and four doors. The drive from Portsmouth to Virginia Beach was about forty-five minutes, and I recall seeing a lot of forests during the drive. We arrived at VA Beach on a Saturday morning, and we planned on being there the entire day, so we brought extra clothes for the evening. Beach clothes during the day while on the beach. I enjoyed the water, while being concerned about jellyfish. It was my first time in the Atlantic Ocean, and I remember thinking I had been in two oceans for the first time within twelve months. I felt a sense of accomplishment for some reason. VA Beach is a fun town and a very long beach walk. The main strip had clubs of all kinds and hamburger joints all over. Souvenir shops and T-shirt shops. I bought my first flip-flops and a T-shirt, but not much more than that. I'm sure I ate a burger, but I don't recall. What I do recall was that evening.

When the sun went down, we showered and changed our clothes at the public shower, just off the beach. We all stowed our beach clothes in the trunk of Mike's car and headed to the VA Beach strip for some fun. It was a pleasant evening that July 1, 1967. It was the beginning of the July 4th celebrations, and the strip was packed with fun people and many groups of very pretty ladies. We were all in good shape, so they would smile at us the same way we smiled at them when we passed several groups. We were all young, and I found myself realizing I was doing something very American for my age that evening. It all felt right, and everyone seemed happy, young, and tanned.

We decided to check out the Peppermint Club right on the strip. It was a big bar room with a small stage on the right as you walked in, and a very long bar on the left. Tables with four chairs spread out in the middle. We grabbed a table near the back and ordered food and cold draft beer in a mug. Bar food basically, but it was good, and we laughed a lot, because we were trying to figure out how to meet one of these nice ladies. I suspect all the nice ladies were trying to figure out the same thing as all the guys as well. The live music show started, and it was great, and at some time during the show, this group of ladies grabbed a table right next to our table. They really seemed interested in meeting us for sure, so we indulged them. They were all from Pittsburgh, and there were seven gals in their group. Fun and ready to have a good time. They were all pretty too. We drank beer and laughed. Mike and I seemed to draw specific interest from two of the ladies. The lady I paired off with and started trying to get to know was named Sonya Brenton, and she lived in Pittsburgh, but now lived here in Virginia Beach with her military family. Her dad was a Navy pilot. I was so impressed with her, and she was beautiful and so funny. I seemed to spend way too much time being fascinated by her name, and for some reason, that became endearing to her and made her laugh. She was nineteen and strong. Not fat at all. Just tall and strong. I liked her accent, and of course she thought my interest in that was funny too. After the show, we all squared up our bill, drank our last beer, and headed out to the boardwalk on the beach. Several of the gals said they were going back to their hotel, and they would meet the other two friends, with me and Mike, later.

We all just sat on a bench on the boardwalk, enjoying the evening. It had gotten a little chilly, but the skies were clear and filled with stars. Sonya asked me to go for a walk on the beach with her, and I told Mike not to leave without me. I told him I would meet him back at his car in an hour, and we agreed.

Walking on the beach with Sonya was nice, and she immediately grabbed my hand, which surprised me, but seemed so pleasant. We walked near the shore for a while, looking at all the lights on the strip behind us. As we decided to turn around and walk back, Sonya squared up with me, face-to-face, and kissed me on the beach in such a nice way. I was with this gorgeous lady, a little older than me, and she was so sweet and beautiful, and I couldn't help but think that this was such a truly romantic moment in my life. I was kissing this beautiful lady on the beach along the Atlantic Ocean. That moment has stuck in my mind, and I will always remember it.

We got back to where Mike and I agreed to meet, which was actually near their hotel. I exchanged mailing address with Sonya, and we said good-bye. I never saw her again. She wrote me for a few months, and then the letters stopped, and my letters didn't receive any further replies.

Mike and I drove off to meet up with the other two guys and get back to Portsmouth. It was 4:30 on Sunday morning, July 2, 1967, and we only had a few more weeks of Pharmacy C-School. I have never been back to VA Beach since that one weekend.

The final week of Pharmacy C-School at Portsmouth was basically waiting for our next orders, or where our next duty station would be. The announcement was coming that Wednesday, August 9th. We were all very interested and wondering where we would be going next week. All the guys were concerned about being deployed with Marines in a war zone, and the ladies seem relaxed because they were never assigned to war zones during that time. They were going to some nice, cozy medical center, anywhere on the globe they put on their "wish list." We were all allowed to complete a duty station wish list, but we were told that there were no guarantees. We understood what they meant, and I thought about that for days prior to the announcement.

I recall an officer and a master chief were in charge in full uniform in the front of the class that day. They spoke briefly and congratulated us as a group for finishing C-School. We were one of the first classes to complete Pharmacy C-School there. Once again, they called individuals up to the front of the class, gave them a certificate, and whispered their orders privately. After we heard our orders, we were instructed to exit the class and proceed to the main office for travel tickets and transportation. It was our last day there, and we were all packed as ordered before class. Things were moving very fast.

They called out about twenty people, including Mike, and then closed the door. They announced that we (me and the nine other guys) were all being deployed for one year with USMC 3rd Infantry Division (3rd-Mar-DIV) to Da Nang, Vietnam. They said, after our one-year tour in Vietnam, we would complete our tour of duty either on board an aircraft carrier or at one of the naval hospitals around the world. I heard what they were saying, but it was coming through to me in a muffled way. I remember looking down at the desk I was sitting at, and watching it spin. I had never felt a more sobering moment in my life, and I don't think I was alone. We were all concerned, but were reminded that we were corpsmen first, and had received FMS training. As they wrapped up, the master chief said, "We know you'll do a good job. The Marines and country need you now. Good luck!"

Are you fucking kidding me, I thought to myself, and shared my feelings by mouthing those same words quietly with a look on my face and my slumped posture to those remaining in the room. We all looked the same.

They told us that they would follow us down to the main office to check out and receive our instructions. I recall being in a daze, trying to recalculate everything I had tried to do in order to avoid this war. I kept thinking I should have known I was going when I was sent to FMS training. That's the facet of my strategy to survive this, I just didn't anticipate. I wasn't totally surprised, but I felt my military service luck had just run out. I immediately started preparing my mind for what was to come. It just seemed really ugly, hard, and so dangerous.

We lined up outside the main office on the first floor. The whole thing was well organized. Everyone was offered two weeks leave to go home before being deployed. When I was offered, I declined, telling the C-School yeoman, third class, I didn't need leave and that I wanted to move on to my next duty station and get it over with. They thought I was upset at first, but the wry smile on my face gave them a sense I was serious and not upset. I was asked three times, "Are you sure?" Each time they asked that, I said, "One hundred percent. Let's do this. I'm ready." They all gave me that "be careful what you wish for" saying and shook their heads. I was given my records and my airline ticket back to San Diego and the Marines at Pendleton. The bus was already waiting outside the building to take everyone to the airport, and as I turned around, the master chief said, "God speed, Kinane." I said, "Thank you, Master Chief," and turned around, hauling my duffle bag and gear to the bus.

I don't remember the bus ride or the flight. I don't recall how I got back to Pendleton, but I met up with my new unit heading over to Vietnam. I received additional Marine green uniforms and boots along with my helmet and flak jacket vest. I was told I would be issued a .45-caliber handgun in-country. We were sailing out of San Diego Bay on the USNS *General Nelson M. Walker* (The Walker), which is a troop transport ship, with over 2,000 men on board, heading in the same direction. I had never seen a ship this big in my life. We were assigned a berthing unit and footlocker. The berthing units were all over the ship. Some four bunks high. Space was tight, and I recall being instructed to meet the chief corpsman at sick bay on board ship. He would give me further instructions.

I stowed my gear and found my way to the nearest head and then over to sick bay, which was on the same deck as my berthing unit. That's where I met Senior Chief Edwards and two other corpsmen assigned to the ship. The ship had a real doctor on board, but only Chief Edwards reported to him, unless he was needed for a surgery. That's what I was told. Chief said there were twenty other corpsmen on board, and that he was going to meet each one that day; we would all muster together at sick bay at 0600 the next morning. We would be assigned to the ship's sick bay for the duration of the transport. This would keep us busy during the voyage and allow him to teach us everything we needed to know while serving Marines in-country. He said he had already served in-country two tours, so he knew what we wanted to know and would share everything we needed to know to survive. I thought, *That's exactly what I need to know, Chief. You seem to know exactly what I'm thinking. Thank goodness I'm reporting to this guy,* I thought. He seemed reasonable. He was from Minnesota and didn't come across as some crazy redneck. He seemed genuinely concerned for all of us. After he reminded us to meet the next morning at 0600, Chief Edwards gave all the new corpsmen being transported the rest of the day off to rest, eat, and try to figure out the ship. It all seemed incredibly cramped and confusing to me. I started looking around the ship. I found the nearest head. I found the chow hall, which was this huge open space on the deck above where my berthing unit was. We were told the trip over would take eight days, depending on weather, so I prepared to make the best of it. I went to chow just before we shoved off. Big mistake. I became seasick right away, and even though I was able to get a dose of Dramamine from the sick bay, I was sick that entire first night, and I wasn't alone. I could hear the moaning and puking all around me. It was a very long night.

The next morning and every morning, I was seasick. I went to the chow hall for some milk and juice. Even that was hard to keep down. When we mustered in front of the sick bay, Chief Edwards had a smile on his face and asked, "Is there anyone not seasick?" He laughed when he didn't get a reply. He said, "Well, this is not unusual, nor is it unexpected. This happens to almost everyone making this journey, so don't worry about it. You guys take it easy, take care of yourselves, and if you need any Dramamine, just come here, and we'll get you guys a daily dose. We'll be on this ship for another week, so do the best you can, but try to make it here as much as you can. I've got a lot of information and details for you, prior to disembarking in Da Nang. On your final day on board, I'm going to issue you your M-5 bags, so make sure you're here next week."

We all said, "Aye, aye, Chief," and headed back to our racks.

I do recall people playing live music and cards all around the ship. Special Services on board ship would lend almost anything to troops in order to break the monotony. When some guys were playing electric guitar on the fantail deck, I went up there briefly to hear. Those guys were actually good, I thought, but it was REALLY crowded, so I went back down. Card games were being played all over, and I joined a couple of games. When real money was brought up, in terms of wagering, I usually folded my hand and walked away. I didn't mind playing cards, but I recall seeing signs posted all over, "No Gambling," and I figured I'd obey this repeated command. I just didn't want to draw any negative attention to myself for any reason. By day five, everyone seemed bored to tears, and for me, eating wasn't appealing, because as soon as the ship would noticeably start rolling, even a little, I was puking in the head for about a half hour. I had almost nothing in my stomach, but I was sick. Even during fire drills, which happened several times during that week-long voyage. We would always muster with our big orange life vest and listen to sailors demonstrate life-saving rescues while standing by our assigned lifeboats on the starboard side of the ship. The fresh air always seemed to help, and looking out, all we could see was water—until we made it a couple of miles off the coast of Da Nang. We could clearly see the shore and what seemed like smoke from fires burning.

This is Vietnam, I thought. *I hope I survive this.*

I was scared, but ready to go, moving forward. I was well trained, I thought, and I had better man up.

Chief Edwards told each one of us where to go, and wished us well. He had assigned all the Navy corpsmen to one landing craft, and we would meet a group of U.S. Marine gunny sergeants on the beach. He told me to go directly to the airfield manifest tent and give my name and number. I said, "Will do, Chief, and thank you for all your help."

"You're welcome, Kinane. You're a good corpsman, and these Marines will be needing you, understand?"

"Yes."

"Kinane, you will be heading to your permanent duty station while you're here in-country. After you manifest, you will be placed on a helicopter and flown north towards Khe Sanh. You're assigned to Charlie Med Base, which is near the Marine outpost in Khe Sanh, and these Marines need your help. Think fast and keep paying attention," Chief Edwards said directly into my ear, under my helmet.

"I understand, Chief." I told him it didn't matter, because I already wasn't sure where I was.

He laughed a little and said, "You'll be fine; just stay positive. You're an E-4, Petty Officer, so more than likely you won't be going on into the bush with a platoon. You'll probably stay the entire time on Charlie Med."

I said, "Got it, Chief. Thank you."

As he turned around, I could hear him say something about the monsoon season, and not to let all the rain and mud bother me. I thought to myself, *I just want to do the best I can and survive this*, and turned around and went to my muster station. I never saw Chief Edwards again. He helped me a lot. He really seemed to care.

It was pouring rain outside on the top deck. Duffle bags were being placed in a separate ship that was being lowered when full. They would get to the beach at least fifteen minutes before any of us on board those landing boats. It seemed well organized, until I found out that each one of us was going over the side on a rope to get into our landing boat. The rope was like a large spiderweb, and extremely unstable. I never enjoyed heights, and I sure did not enjoy this, but I started down the rope-ladder with everyone going over the side of the ship. The landing boats were the same type of boats they used during WWII on D-Day and Iwo Jima. Just a little larger and newer. As I descended the rope, I can remember thinking, *How the fuck did you get here, Charlie?* I slowly, carefully, and deliberately started moving down the rope, step by step, and holding on for dear life. The pack on my back and my flak jacket made it even harder. I finally got to the last step and had a hard time releasing from the rope, finally jumping the few extra feet down to the deck of the landing craft. I was one of the last ones to board, and the boat was already rocking more than the ship as we bounced repeatedly into the hull of the *Walker*.

We were all packed in and headed towards the beach. I was standing on the port side, towards the rear with a couple other Navy corpsmen. Nobody was talking. We were all just listening while the boat was rocking in the three-foot waves and getting closer to the beach. We were told we would disembark in about three feet of beach water and move directly to the beach, then muster for head count. I just listened and kept my head down. I could see and sometimes only hear guys getting seasick all around me. I was dry-heaving the entire time, spitting off to my side. I wondered how long it would take to get off this boat.

The boat came to a stop, and the engines were running

high. The front gate went down into the water, and we were told over and over, "MOVE FORWARD! MOVE FORWARD! MOVE FORWARD!" At the gate, we were told, "Watch your step and move forward to the beach." I was one of the last off the boat, and as soon as the water went above my boots, it felt warm. There was so much noise, and people screaming at us from all directions. "This way! Come this way!" The loud voices were coming from Marines on the beach. They all sounded like gunnys the way they gave commands. Their voices were definitely strained and hoarse. I moved through the shallow water the twenty yards to the beach. Most of the guys who landed with me were already lining up on the beach. As soon as I stepped out of the water, one of the gunnys on the beach said, "Welcome to Da Nang, Doc! Line up over here quickly. You okay?"

I said, "Yes, I'm fine."

The sand was warm and dry. Again, I was the final one to get in line.

The lead gunny said, "First of all, welcome to Da Nang, Vietnam. This is the northeast coast of South Vietnam, and you are in One Corp. Two Corp is just south of us. Three Corp (Saigon) is just south of Two Corp, and Four Corp is just south of Three Corp, near the Delta. This is the war zone. Listen to everything from those in command at all times. You will be getting your sea legs back to land legs soon. Most of you have been sick, and we know this. You might already be feeling better now, but if not, you will in a couple hours. If not, then go to your sick bay. Your feet are wet from coming ashore, so make sure as soon as you get a chance to change your socks.

Keep your feet as dry as possible here. It won't be easy, but protect your feet.

"Corpsman Petty Officer Kinane, why do we keep our feet dry?"

I was stunned he knew my name, but I shouted back, "Trench foot, Gunny!"

He barked back, "Repeat that, Kinane."

"Trench foot, Gunny!"

"That's right." Then he said, "I'm going to call your name, and I need you to listen and respond. We don't want to be on this beach too long. It's too open, so listen." He looked down at his clipboard and started calling out names. Each person responded loudly when they heard their name called. The gunny called my name last, and after I responded, he said, "Kinane, you see me after this group is dismissed."

I said, "Roger that."

He explained that a truck would take all of us directly to Da Nang Air Base for further orders and platoon assignments if needed. He told us that it was a short ride in a troop carrier from here to there, and then he dismissed us to the waiting trucks. He walked straight up to me and said, "Kinane, you will be going with me. You're needed at Charlie Med near Khe Sanh. I will get you on a chopper right away. Is that understood?"

"Understood, but could I hit the head somewhere?" I asked.

"There's one near the runway; now go and get in my vehicle," which was a nearby jeep.

Everything was moving really fast. I wondered why I was getting so lucky with all this attention.

I got to the jeep and stood near the rear, because I wasn't sure where I was supposed to sit. All three beach gunnys came toward the jeep, and I was told to sit up front, shotgun. I got in as quickly as I could. Before the engine was started, I couldn't help thinking, *Wow, I'm really in a jeep.* It was my first time, and I thought it was pretty cool. As we took off, the lead gunny, who was driving, started talking to me so I knew what to expect. He told me that getting me up there was a priority, because they were having a hard time keeping inventory of drugs and medical supplies under control. He told me he was up there one time, and that it was north, and not too far from the western border. The Marine outpost was just north of Charlie Med and was constantly taking a beating, and kicking ass back. I just listened. He gave me some paperwork and told me this was my new mailing address and that mail would take three to four weeks to catch up to me. The paperwork included the name of the commanding officer and the name of the chief corpsman. He said there were actually a few female nurses up there. I just listened and nodded my head. It was really loud, so I was trying to focus on everything he was telling me. I didn't have any questions, because I didn't know what to ask. I always wanted to listen more and ask only a few questions. Most times, if you listen carefully, questions you have will be answered before you need to verbalize. Sometimes. Anyway, I was listening to every word being spoken by all three of the gunnys in the jeep.

It took about fifteen minutes to get to the manifest muster tent near the air strip, and as soon as we stopped, one of the gunnys said, "We'll take you to the head, Doc. We got to go too." I followed the two of them and was relieved as soon as I could get "Little Charlie" out of my zipper. It was a wooden building with steps and about ten holes for pissing into or sitting down to take a crap. It wasn't clean at all and smelled so bad. When I was done, all three were waiting for me.

They gave me a manila envelope they said was not to be opened, but to be hand delivered to the base CO… They wished me well and told me to turn around and board the Huey. The Huey would take me directly to Charlie Med, and the trip would take about forty-five minutes. I said, "Thank you," and turned around and saw the helicopter with guys leaning out motioning for me to come on board. "Double time," I heard one of them say. I started jogging quickly, and as soon as I got under the propeller above, I was almost blown over by the wind, but I kept moving towards the door. I put one foot on the skid, and I felt myself pulled into the ship. They told me where to sit and said, "Strap in." As soon as I clicked my seat belt, I felt the ship move and hover. It was a really strange sensation. We started heading northwest, and flew at treetop levels the entire way.

What I could see and hear from my seat were two door gunners with M60 7.62mm MGs. Each door gunner pointed their very deadly and loud weapons out the open door of the helicopter. Both were manning those guns and began firing the weapons down with about ten bursts, while swinging the M60 forward and aft as we flew. I was wondering if this was necessary or if they were practicing. They fired at least a dozen times during the flight. It was fascinating to me. For some reason, watching them fire their weapons didn't bother me. I was very impressed with their courage, and the actual weapon. They seemed hard core to me, so I didn't ask, but they seemed very serious and consumed about their jobs. I just watched them for a while. I was facing backward from the front of the helicopter, so I couldn't see forward. I could see the landscape go by outside each door. I could tell when we seemed to be in a forest, or jungle, and when we seemed to be over open spaces and farms, or rice paddy fields. I noticed a lot of brown spots all over the ground.

The flight was amazing to me. After the first fifteen minutes, I tried to close my eyes and rest for the remainder of this flight to Charlie Med. Just as I was about to close my eyes, I realized there were four others Marines on board. We all looked at each other and nodded. They all smiled and laughed at how "green" I must have looked. I couldn't figure out their rank, but they looked like seasoned Marine officers.

You either got to Charlie Med, or Khe Sanh, by helicopter, foot, humping, or in a tank. Charlie Med was medical support for over 4,000 Marines at the Khe Sanh fire base, just north of Charlie Med, and they were right near the northwest border of south Vietnam, near the DMZ. These Marines were fighting and being fired upon every day. All of those Marines who served there were simply incredible. Such courage, and truly badass. The only other way to Charlie Med was by helicopter, and it was the quickest way to get there. Just then, I wondered, *Am I replacing some corpsman who has been KIA? Why am I needed here so badly? Just go with it. You're here for a year.*

I wasn't sure exactly what date it was, but it was the end of August 1967. I remembered that, because I wanted to keep track of my one-year tour so I knew when it would end next year. If I survived, I was going to hold them to this one-year thing.

The ship was slowing down, and I could feel it starting to descend; I could see Charlie Med outside. It was all dirt, with a big open space and bunkers covered with dirt. The biggest mound of dirt was the medical bunker, where everything happened. Surgery, X-rays, exams, etc. It was a large earthen berm, covered with dirt and sandbags. There was a lot of open space in between the landing zone and the medical bunker. As soon as we landed, we quickly left the Huey. As I was jumping off, there were several Marines putting stretchers on the ship. I could clearly see what was on the stretchers. Bodies in body bags. They placed five bodies on the ship, and the ship took off, creating a huge dust storm. One of the Marine officers on board told me to follow them, and we walked past the big berm on the left and beyond the medical bunker. We were double-timing, and I was following. We entered the bunker just beyond the main large medical bunker, through a dug-out trench lined with sandbags. It got dark just before the electric lights strung up on the posts holding the top of the bunkers illuminated the rooms. There were two large open rooms. On the right as I walked in was a group of desks, and that's where I was told to sit and change my socks. The Marine told me this was the Tactical Operation Command (TOC), and that someone would see me ASAP. He said, while pointing, "Over there is the chow hall and chapel."

I said, "Roger that, sir," and he walked farther down the bunker, where some people met him. While he was talking, he kept pointing over towards me. I began to break down my boots and change my socks. Before putting on one of the two fresh, dry pair of socks I was trained to keep in my pocket, I was thinking about food and wondering when the next chow was. I knew I had C-rations, but it was always worth waiting a little before dealing with that, because I was hungry. I sure was hungry though.

I sat there for about fifteen minutes, watching soldiers pass me by, heading back towards the main medical bunker. Some were going past the other way, but I think it was still morning, and I wondered where they were headed, because as they passed those officers talking about forty yards away on the other side of this big bunker, they would disappear down another bunker somewhere. I wondered where, and remember starting to smell food. *That's always a good thing*, I thought. I sure was hungry after being seasick for over a week.

Finally, someone came up from behind me and tapped me on the shoulder. I stood up and turned towards him. He was clearly a doctor with the stethoscope and the white coat, stained with blood on the sides. He was tall and much older than I was. I guessed maybe thirty-five or forty. He said, "Petty Officer Kinane?"

I said, "Yes, sir," and I was about to salute.

He said, "Please don't salute here. I'm Navy Commander Doctor J.H. Pitt, the commanding officer on this base. You understand that, Kinane?"

I said, "Yes, sir."

"I'm also chief surgeon," he went on to say. "I was wondering what was taking you so long to get here, because I requested you three or four weeks ago. We've got problems with our medical supplies and inventory. Specifically, we have had several incidents of controlled meds disappear, and that must stop."

"Yes sir."

"I will assign someone to you for a complete tour of the base after I dismiss you today. This is my executive officer, Lt. Commander Granato, and he is also a surgeon, but he's also my right-hand man here on all levels. If he tells you something, it's coming from me."

Lt. Commander Granato was a tall man with dark hair. I wasn't sure if he was Italian or Mexican, but I could tell he was confident, with a good smile. He seemed cool right off the bat. I said, "Nice to meet you, sir."

He nodded back. "We really need you here, Petty Officer Kinane."

Commander Pitt continued to explain some things, and added, "Afternoon chow will be served for one hour starting in about ten minutes, so you grab some food as soon as they open. I need you to answer these questions at this desk by the time I get back here in about two hours." He handed me a paper with several questions.

I looked at it quickly and said, "Yes, sir."

"This is the quickest and most efficient way for me to get to know you and your skills. There's no wrong answer, Kinane. I already know a lot about you, but this will help me. Understood?"

I said, "Yes, sir," and he turned around and headed back

toward the main medical tent.

Lt Commander Granato said, "Make sure to get some food, Kinane. We know you're hungry." He smiled and followed Pitt. I sat down, grabbed my pencil, and started reading the questions.

I had just finished reading over the one-sided paper with all the questions when a female soldier walked up to me. "Hi, I'm Lt. Cranfit, and I'm the head nurse here on base. Why don't you come with me and have some chow? They're about to serve, and it's customary to line up."

"Yes, ma'am, I'm hungry."

She asked, "Why so hungry?"

I replied, "I was sick the entire voyage over here from San Diego, and it's been hard to keep anything down. I think I've got my land legs back now, ma'am."

"Didn't you eat after you landed?"

"No, ma'am, I was immediately on a chopper right after hitting the beach. I haven't eaten a real meal since being on board ship yesterday."

She said she understood, chuckled, and asked, "Did you change your socks?"

"Yes, ma'am, thank you."

We got in line just as it started moving. She told me that today was in-processing for me and after speaking with the CO in a few hours, I would get a tour of the base and where I would be sleeping. She told me that it was busy here and that I should relax, follow orders, and remember my training. I had been selected to come here sometime late July of that year. My records so far were outstanding, and they needed someone like me to get a handle on control meds and medical supplies and all that inventory. She told me there were always around fifty Marines, corpsmen, and officers stationed here for their year in-country. Of those fifty, there were two other women, both nurses and both naval officers like her.

She said, "You will meet everyone here soon, because your position on this base is important, and the CO and generals are confident you'll get this all squared away."

I said, "Yes, ma'am," and we had our trays in our hands and were being served hot food. The meal was excellent. When you are as hungry as I was at that moment, an old leather boot, with a little seasoning on it, would have tasted good. We finished our meals, tossed our trash, and placed our trays on a rack near the trash. I realized Lt. Cranfit really didn't talk much, and I didn't recall anyone talking to her at all. I passed it off as that's how she ate or took breaks. She just seemed cold during our twenty-minute meal. When we got back to my gear near the desk, she said, "You know where the head is, right?"

I said, "Yes, ma'am, I saw the signs. Thank you."

"Complete the form for the CO, and he should be here within forty-five minutes." She didn't say good-bye. She just turned around on her heels and walked toward the main medical tent or bunker. After that first great meal, I actually felt good for the first time in days. *I'm here. Survive,* I was thinking. *You'll survive.* I repeated the thought in my head. I started answering the list of questions on the sheet.

The sheet was a welcome from the CO, Navy Commander J.H. Pitt, MD. He gave a list of all his staff on the left, and on top explained how to complete the one-sided form. At the bottom of the form was our mailing address and his message about mail. "All mail is welcome, and when it comes, it will get priority, so it will get to you. Whatever mail you might be anticipating at arrival might take a few weeks, but your mail will get here." It was an APO address. I took note of it in my notebook. The questions were to be answered this way: My Skills Are Strong. My Skills Are Passable. My Skills Are Week. They were in columns, and I was to check one of the three for my training skills: A & P, drawing blood, BP & P, ratio & proportion, triage selection, injections, suturing, compounding (creams, ointments, elixirs, IVs), starting IV, tourniquet, math, Latin medical abbreviations, unit dose, weapons, inventory, ordering, environmental hazards (malaria, trench foot, leaches, scabies), delousing, burns, nausea, morphine, antibiotics, and a few other questions I can't recall. I checked off "Strong" for everything except suturing. I had been trained to suture, but I had to admit, my training did not go well.

I finished in about fifteen minutes, giving each checkmark careful consideration, but I was being honest, and I figured while I'm here, I might as well be really busy, and perhaps I'd avoid direct combat. I was hoping anyway. I also kept thinking *I hope to God I never am called to suture.*

After about an hour and a half, Lt. Commander Pitt came back to the desk alone. He sat in the far more comfortable chair and said, "Welcome to my office, Kinane, and more than that, welcome to Third Medical Battalion, Third Marine

Division (reinforced). We really need you here, young man, and I'm expecting a lot of good things from you."

I said, "Yes, sir, I'll do my best."

"I know you will, and I'll be doing a lot of your important training myself tomorrow after morning chow, at 0715. Roger that?" he said, looking up at me from the paper with the questions.

I said, "Roger, sir."

He kept looking at the paper for about five minutes, every now and then looking up at me across the desk. I felt he was really sizing me up. He looked up and said, "Thank you for completing this. It saves me a lot of time getting to know you and what you can do or what you feel strong about. All of this is important to this command."

"Yes, sir."

"Listen, I'm always busy, and my time is highly in demand here, so understand I move fast, but carefully. You'll have to get up to speed with the rhythm and demand of being a crucial member of this command. I don't anticipate you ever going out in the bush with a Marine platoon, but each platoon needs at least one corpsman in order to go out. We have fourteen and now with you, fifteen corpsmen now at this command, and you did get your chevron at the end of C-School, so you do have some rank as an NCO, and your mission here is different. Heavy on inventory control, especially our controlled meds. Drug abuse has become a problem with troops here, and the President and General Westmoreland want this drug problem in Vietnam solved, and under control on all commands. You'll be asked to participate and respond to commands in surgery. You'll assist moving wounded on stretchers and moving KIA on stretchers to the cemetery area. You will be called upon for triage. You will have some duty time at sick bay. I want to emphasize that I can't guarantee you won't go into the bush with an M-16, along with your .45, but I really doubt that will happen. If it does, know that it was a difficult decision to make, but it came from me. You'll figure out what you're doing over the next weeks or so, but you'll be putting in no less than twelve-hour work days. You'll get your time in the rack, but sometimes you're awake and working for twenty-four hours because it's just that busy. Downtime always happens, but when the shit hits the fan here, you'll understand what I mean. Always keep your helmet and flak jacket near you, along with your .45. Clear the chamber any-time you enter a bunker. Is all this understood?"

I said, "Yes, sir. I'm ready to get working."

He said, "Outstanding, and if you're fucking up and not able to grasp something, your only warning will be from me, and that is this: Don't fuck up again...understood?"

"Yes, sir."

He told me to gather my gear and meet the Marine in front of the NCO bunker. "That's where you'll set up rack and stow your gear." As he left he added, "Be on time tomorrow at 0715 and take care of your feet."

My head was spinning, but I kept thinking, *I hope I don't go into the bush. I just made it here.* I gathered my gear and start-ed walking away from the main medical bunker toward the NCO bunker and other bunkers. Signs were everywhere. This bunker this way. Male shower and latrine/head this way. Female shower and latrine/head this way. Signs pointed everywhere, and there were several signs about feet. I finally had to laugh about the feet, but they were so right.

I signed into my bunker, and I was shown where my rack would be. The room was dark, musty, and had one dim lightbulb hanging from the middle of the room near the wooden ceiling. There were six bunks, lined up three on each side, and it appeared only two were currently being used. They were taken near the rear of the bunker. The occupants had somehow rigged curtains around their bunk areas, like it was an emergency room in a hospital. No totally private, but private enough. I took the bunk near the door on the left side. I figured I would have as much space for myself as possible. As I was making that final decision, I thought about the noise of people walking past the front of the bunker and figured if it was too bad, I would try to make some change. I never did change that sleeping spot in that bunker.

I pulled out all the gear and clothing from my duffle bag and placed it all in the three drawers on the metal nightstand near my desk. The linens were placed on the rack by the Marine who showed me the bunker, so I made the bed and put the pillowcase on my pillow. I felt lucky to have a bunk at that time. Since evening chow wasn't for a couple more hours, I decided to lie down and take a nap. I fell asleep quickly.

When I woke up, I could hear the two other bunker mates talking about chow. They welcomed me and came over to introduce themselves. Both guys were corpsmen and 3rd class petty officers, just like me. One black guy was C.N. Branch from New Jersey, and the other guy's name was Issabella (Izzy) Thompson from Pennsylvania. Friendly guys who had been here for a few months. Branch had been here for almost ten months and was counting the days down, waiting for his day to demobilize (d-mob), sometime in November. They immediately asked me if I was going to chow, and I said yes, and I was up and walking back towards the chow hall where I ate with Lt. Cranfit. On the way there, they told me everyone was talking about me and my lunch with "Cranflake." I thought, *Oh, oh, what's up with her?*

Chow was prepared and served by Marine cooks, and they were good. They served basic American food, or whatever food supplies were available. As I went through the chow line with my tray, I couldn't help but notice the stacks and stacks of C-ration boxes behind each server, trying to keep all the food warm or chilled. They served three meals three times each day, if possible. The chow line was only available for thirty minutes, and it served about forty to fifty people per meal. It wasn't the Ritz, but these Marines took great pride in their mission, and by doing a great job, they stayed on the base. The food was usually good, and hot. Coffee, Coke, water, milk, and juice were available to drink, and they were kept in a large fridge with a window so you could see what was in there. Second helpings were frowned upon, and the sign behind the serving line stated that too. There were roughly ten six-man picnic tables to eat on Charlie Med.

I sat down with Branch and Izzy, and I followed them as they said a quick prayer before eating. They started giving me the low down on what life was like here at Charlie Med. They told me what the hard jobs were and what jobs were routine. They started talking about how many times they had worked over twenty-four hours in a row, and how bad some days were in terms of wounded, KIA, and being under direct attack. They told me CO Pitt was really cool and really smart, and that Lt Commander Granato was really cool too. They said the two other nurses were always either in the main medical bunker or the recovery bunker. They both agreed that they were hardworking, professional, and pleasant. Both were engaged to guys in the military, but they were never sure where or what branch. That was just the word about them. They didn't flirt, but they enjoyed laughing every now and then. Then they started to tell me about Cranfit, who they called "Cranflake." They told me she was a back stabber and not to be trusted. She thought she was better than anyone below her rank, especially enlisted. They said she kissed all the doctors' asses, and especially CO Pitt. They encouraged me to watch out for her and to keep my distance at all costs. She was apparently a snake. I guessed that answered my question about nobody talking with her during noon chow earlier that day. I made a huge mental note of that.

They said we call our sleeping bunker a hooch, but there were no so-called "Mamasans" to clean up. They simply and respectfully asked me to try to keep things clean and organized. I said, "No problem with that."

After chow, Branch and Izzy took me outside so they could smoke and show me as much of the base and facilities on base as possible. There were approximately fifty Marines handling security on the base, while 4,000 Marines were at the fire base not too far away. Charlie Med wasn't a big base, but there were always helicopters landing and taking off. The landing zone could land two Hueys at a time, or one big Chinook by itself. Chinooks were usually moving troops or bringing in provisions and supplies and mail.

Branch and Izzy said there was typically a movie being shown around eight each night, unless it was too busy or we were under direct attack. I thought that was cool about the movies, but what was being under attack like? I had a feeling I would find that out personally soon enough. Marines were guarding the only gate and the entire wire twenty-four/seven. Each day or two, fifteen to twenty Marines and one corpsman would go out into the bush nearby on search-and-destroy missions. That was considered "attack prevention," and apparently it worked, because attacks did happen, but not too often. The Marines usually cleaned out a perimeter outside our wire for about a mile all around, and they usually engaged the enemy two or three times a week. They said, nine times out of ten, when Marines engaged outside the wire, there were casualties returning. That's when it got really busy. We went back to the chow hall, which had been converted to a small movie theater. Tonight's show was the first showing of *Bonnie and Clyde*, and they knew seats would be taken because of all the hype about the movie. The movie started exactly at 2000 (8:00 p.m.) and ended around 2200. It was the most exciting time I had ever had watching a film. After the film, I hit my rack, and so did Branch and Izzy. I thought these were good guys, and I had told them what I was doing at 0715 the next morning with CO Pitt. They didn't know anything about it, and we all went to sleep, but they did say they would set me up with some curtains to put around my rack the next day. It was like sleeping in a noisy hotel.

I woke up at 0600 and walked to the nearby shower/head. I quickly S.S.S., and headed to chow, which started serving at 0700. I was first in line because I didn't want to be late for the 0715 meeting with CO Pitt. Being late in the Navy was considered Unauthorized Absence (UA), and I figured I would avoid any type of negative report about me that included UA in the report. I knew that was something I could clearly avoid. I was rarely late for anything, even before being drafted. I seemed obsessed with being on time and didn't mind waiting when I was early.

I saw CO Pitt eating his breakfast with some troops a few tables away, and he saw me getting up from my chow spot and heading to the supply bunker. I got to the supply bunker at least five minutes before CO Pitt and waited. It was a large bunker with a big metal lock on the door. CO Pitt showed up and opened the door with his key. He said there were only two keys to this lock, and that I was getting one today. He opened the door and turned on the one overhead light. There were no windows, so it was still dim inside the room. The room was in complete disarray, with supplies opened and empty boxes all over the floor. There were two large refrigerators running on one side, a big table in the middle, and shelves of supplies lining every inch of the bunker's inside. It was a real mess.

Just as CO Pitt started talking to me about the room, we heard an explosion. It wasn't close, but it was heard. He immediately said, "That's incoming, so let's get down. Five more explosions followed. Two seemed close, and very loud. The two close explosions shook the ground, and loose dirt fell from the top of the bunker. CO Pitt said, "That's a typical mortar attack, Kinane. Get used to that. When that happens, follow orders, or if you're alone, do exactly what we just did right now, and cover. You'll be fine. That was nothing compared to some of the attacks we have had the last few months." He went on to tell me that Marines guarded the perimeter and wire, and they were really good at their jobs. Apparently, "the enemy," as he called them, got onto the base twice, but were neutralized quickly by Marine guards. He continued to tell me about my job and what he expected.

CO Pitt told me to begin organizing and detailing the entire room. He said, "Get everything in order here, and I'll be back around noon chow to see how you're doing."

I said, "Yes, sir," and he quickly left, after saying, "Good, I'll see you later, Kinane."

I looked around and tried to figure out where to start. I was knee deep in empty boxes of medical supplies, and shelves so out of control, with half-empty boxes and papers and box wrappers everywhere. I had about four hours to get something done for the CO, and so I just started breaking down empty boxes. I was very happy to be doing something that needed to be done, and this was simple enough for a start.

CO Pitt came back just before noon chow and looked at the room with amazement. Somehow, he was able to create this glow with his happy face and body language, obviously impressed with my job. He kept looking back at me, pointing at an area now squared away, and smiling. "Good job, Kinane. Outstanding. You work fast too. Do you feel you're completely finished organizing this room?" he asked me.

I said, "Well, sir, I'd like to label where each supply is now. I've got it an alpha sequence by product now, but I'd like to apply labels so we can find each supply quicker. I did the same in the fridge, and I would like to create some simple form of labeling. I think it would make this room and the use of this room far more efficient, but I would need a few more hours to accomplish this, sir."

"Do it, Kinane, and let's sit down and talk about this while we're eating. You ready?"

"Yes, sir. I'm hungry."

It was over that quick meal that CO Pitt told me what he expected from me, and what he wanted me to do within his command. My job was all supplies, with full priority on medical supplies. Aside from XO Granato and the CO himself, I was the only person with a key to this supply room. He told me he was putting me in a position that required high trust, and that I was responsible for guarding, keeping, providing, and ordering all medical supplies and other supplies needed for the base other than food. I would have nothing to do with ordering food or C-rations.

"The Marine combat cooks will take care of all that." He paused. "Control medications are to be guarded vigorously, Kinane. We had a horrible problem a couple months ago, and it involved missing controlled medications. We're not sure, but we think it may have been one or two of our local interpreters on base at the time. We replaced each one, and you'll see them on base while you're here. Sadly, there are not enough trained South Vietnamese soldiers to have stationed here. We're fighting for them and their country here at Charlie Med. You may see one at triage, or in recovery if they get wounded or become casualties, so don't be surprised when you do see one of the dozen we have. They're all pleasant and speak English and Vietnamese. They will speak to you only in English. Anyway, we can't allow theft to happen here, ever again, or it's my ass. Now, it will also be yours if something happens. Is that completely understood, Kinane?"

I said, "Yes, sir. Roger Wilco."

He smiled and said, "Good. I've got to get back to my team of surgeons now. I'll see you before evening chow today. Go back to work."

"Yes, sir."

I put my tray back and went back to work organizing that supply room.

Over time, CO Pitt would add to my duties. He had me ordering everything his team needed in terms of supplies. He had me ordering meds, including control meds, which required his signature. At first he co-signed all my request chits, but after a few weeks, just the meds. I was able to make the room work really well, and I had an extra lock installed on the door. I got to the point where I would find a window (downtime) in the surgery bunker and recovery bunker and simply look at what they need, and I would bring it to them and stock it, even before someone would come to the supply room asking for that supply. Pitt always seemed impressed, and when he was, he would just nod or give me the thumbs-up sign. He would always say hello when we passed each other, and I started to become really impressed with him and how he ran this base. He was confident, and he was so freaking smart. Every person on the base admired him and had tremendous respect for him.

After a couple of months, sometime late October 1967, he asked me to begin participating in the triage staging area. Mostly starting IV's and administering morphine as directed. I also participated in unloading helicopters and bringing in supplies I had requested. I was the only person, other than Pitt and Granato, who could receive and accept any medications. They were usually in chilled foam containers, so you knew, and the guys delivering it knew as well. It was always good to be outside of the bunkers, but never for too long, because of intel suggesting snipers in the area outside the wire. I never minded jumping in on anything I was ordered to do by Pitt, and keeping busy really passed the time quickly.

After about six weeks, I did meet some of the Vietnamese soldier/interpreters. One particular interpreter seemed genuinely friendly. His name was Phuc Mi Kim. He understood why people would laugh when they heard his name, but that was his name. He was a gentle, smart, and reflective soul. He was the lead interpreter on base, and when with the other interpreters, he was as highly regarded as CO Pitt by his men. His leadership skills were strong, and he never asked one of the other interpreters to do anything he wouldn't do himself. He went out on many search-and-destroy missions with Marines. He had survived many combat battles out in the bush with Marines and never seemed rattled on the outside. There was a serious and reflective nature about him, but he enjoyed a good laugh from time to time. I told him I would call him "Kim." He said, "Good," after we had gotten to know each other. I found out that he was thirty-four years old and that he had lost his entire family four years earlier. He didn't talk much, unless he had to, but he was a really good man. I was so impressed with his courage and strength. We shared many meals together at Charlie Med.

After I got used to my day-to-day routine, I asked CO Pitt if I could help out at triage, staging, and he agreed, as long as my job was under control. From about mid-October 1967 on, I would listen to the helicopter pilots on the radio, coming to the base. They would describe the number of casualties on board and the situation in the air. Sometimes they would be taking fire as they left the combat zone landing zone (LZ). You could easily tell by the stress in their voices when their ship was taking fire. Even the really cool, calm pilots would have a more urgent sound to their radio voice. These pilots were extraordinary in terms of their courage and training. I was always in awe when listening to those radio calls.

As they would report their numbers of casualties, I would prepare the number of bottles of IVs and individual doses of morphine I anticipated being needed. I always made sure I had at least one extra bottle, and dose, just in case the number was low being reported. I didn't want to be out there starting IVs and giving morphine to those who needed it, and run out with one troop still in need of help.

The triage/staging area was about forty feet by forty feet, and it was outside the main medical bunker. If there was only one or two casualties, they would each be brought into the surgical portion of the medical bunker. If there were more than two, at least one would remain at the staging until the doctors, surgeons, and nurses were ready. Rain or shine, and I think it rained every day I was in Vietnam. Night or day. We never knew when the helicopters would come in, but we always had about fifteen minutes to be ready. During my time at Charlie Med, we saw hundreds of Marine casualties, if not more than a thousand. Days without incoming casualties were few and far between, but we did have a day or two when no casualties would land at our LZ on base. It was loud and busy, and you could easily tell the difference between every other helicopter and a Chinook. Chinooks shook everything and seem to hover longer, just above our bunkers. Dust would fly inside each sandbag-reinforced bunker, which always seemed like a manmade cave on those occasions. Hueys seemed to be able to move troops quickly in and out of the combat zone just north of our base, so they were the types of helicopters that would land when casualties were involved.

The idea at Charlie Med, and on the staging area, was to implement this triage system, and stick with it, because we needed some system to try to keep these wounded alive and save limbs. There was always quite a bit of screaming, groaning, and crying at the staging area. I recall injecting so many troops with morphine, based upon the surgical warrant officer's (physician's assistant, and I don't recall his name) assessment of each wounded Marine lying on a stretcher. In some cases, CO Pitt or XO Granato would attach the eight-by-ten white card on their chests with instructions for IV and whether they needed morphine or not. Most needed it, and I was happy to inject. I had never had morphine myself, but I knew that upon injection, the wounded Marine would feel flush and start to relax. The pain at the location of the injury or wound would never go away while they were on their stretchers, and I would explain to them what the morphine would do and tell them to try to relax and not move. We would get to them as quickly as possible. They would always ask, "How long, Doc?" I would tell them soon, because I never really knew, but I knew based upon what I had already seen, they would be out there in staging for less than a half hour. To them, it may have seemed like an eternity, but based on what we were up against treating them, we got to them quickly. One time we had ten or eleven come in, and they were all wounded. Pitt had this so efficiently managed, all things considered. I recall we were able to get all ten or eleven of those wounded Marines off the staging area and into surgery within ten minutes. We had a well-trained unit, and I was proud to be in a position to actually help. I felt I had become a small, yet important part of the base mission. I understood what the CO was trying to do, and it all made sense to me.

Lt. Cranflake was a totally different story. She was always in the face of every corpsman on the base. Sometimes for the most minor issues, like dropping a piece of paper that was once the wrapper for bandages. One time, I watched her dress down a corpsman for not arriving to a meal at the proper time. I thought she was petty, and just because I felt Pitt was totally on my side and cared about me, she didn't spare her crazy power trip on me. She always wanted to come inside the storage room and tell me how to organize everything, despite the CO telling me he liked it and didn't want it to change. She would give me grief anyway. I was told that prior to my arrival at Charlie Med, she was in charge of supplies for the CO, and I recall how long it took me to get everything under control, including all medical supply orders. She always seemed to have her nose in everything I did and tried to make weird changes to the orders, even after Pitt had signed the chit. After the first time she tried to change the order, I would not allow her to see any further orders after Pitt had signed off on them. Cranflake was just miserable, and her miserable nature wasn't helping anyone.

Cranflake would dress down any soldier with the most minor, petty issue. She was always playing the "I outrank you" card. This included her two nurse officers on base, who were hardworking and down-to-earth professionals. Lt. Junior Grade Martin, who was a wonderful black lady, and Lt. Junior Grade Lynne were often victims of her irrational wrath. Usually, she would dress them down loudly for something that happened or didn't happen during a surgery. It was embarrassing to see this happen to two of the most dedicated and compassionate Navy officers I think I have ever known. They were nice people, and they kept to themselves. They didn't talk much because they were always busy in the surgical bunker or the recovery bunker with other corpsmen and troops stabilizing before being transported to a large facility. Don't get me wrong, Cranflake seemed to work hard too, but she just didn't seem to understand where we were for some reason, and she thought simply because of her rank, she was better than anyone below her rank, especially enlisted. Even NCOs. I realized after about a month, I wanted nothing to do with her, and I wasn't alone in that strategy of avoiding her every minute of every day on Charlie Med. She was a big negative, and there was even casual talk of fragging her.

Whenever I heard about some idea of fragging anyone, I tried to shift the conversation back to what we were up against and who we were really fighting. Fragging is basically murdering someone and making it look like it was the enemy who did it. I wasn't going to submit to any discussion of this, and to my knowledge, and within my perimeter, fragging never happened. I knew it did happen, but I wasn't going to condone it, and I wasn't going to be involved with one. I simply wanted to survive and try to keep everyone I could alive. Cranflake was a problem, but I knew Pitt was making notes and talking to her regularly. Maybe he wanted her to be the "bad cop" on base, I thought. Maybe he didn't like her either, but really needed her on staff. I'm not sure, but regardless of all her meetings with Pitt, she was always a bitch. I felt she was a climber, and climbers who were obvious about their "climbing the ranks" desire made me sick and annoyed. Ass-kissing, to me, was disgusting and wrong. Be pleasant, but be aware of when pleasant crosses over into ass-kissing. She didn't seem to have any self-awareness.

Sometime around Halloween, or maybe exactly on Halloween, 1967, interpreter Kim brought a little dog to me and asked if I wanted it. I wasn't sure about the base policy, but I told him I would ask CO Pitt if I could keep the little brown dog with the white patch on her chest and the one white paw. I could tell immediately that she liked me because when Kim gave her to me so I could hold her, she started climbing all over me and kissing my face and arms. She weighed about ten pounds, I estimated, and she was over a year old. She wasn't a puppy, but she was young and thin. I asked Kim if she had a name, and he said, "Her name is Di Di Mau." I laughed so hard about her name and fell more in love with her at that moment. As soon as Kim took her back to his bunker, I locked up the supply room and walked towards the TOC, where CO Pitt was completing forms at his desk.

This was one of the rare moments I actually went up to CO Pitt as he was working at his desk. I didn't like to bother him, and everyone respected his incredibly busy schedule. I stood in front of his desk for about thirty seconds before he looked up and said, "What do you need, Kinane?"

I said, "Sir, I have been given the opportunity to have a small pet dog, and would like to keep her as long as you approve."

He asked me some questions about the dog and said, "I don't mind, as long as your hooch mates, Izzy and Branch, don't mind. Also, if someone takes one of those three open racks in your hooch, you must get that person's permission too."

I said, "Thank you, sir," turned around sharply, and went towards Kim's hooch/bunker to get my new dog. CO Pitt smiled slightly and put his head back down into the pile of forms and records he was reviewing or filling out.

Di Di Mau and I got along great, and everyone on the base who saw her seemed to fall in love with her too. She barely made a sound and was terrified when the base came under mortar or rocket attacks. She would hide under the covers on my rack, or try to sneak under the rack. I fed her twice a day, after morning chow and afternoon chow. She never did her business inside a bunker. Somehow, she always gave me a look that told me she had to go, and I always got her out-side, near the men's head and shower bunker. I would always clean up her poop. She was the perfect dog, and I hoped that she would come home with me when I demobilized out of Vietnam. She was my first dog, and Kim was kind enough to give me a real champ. We were inseparable there at Charlie Med, and she gave me a sense of peace each day; peaceful moments in the war zone before adopting her were not as relaxed for some reason. This little dog gave me such a wonderful peace.

On several occasions, I was called to resupply the surgical room when surgeries were going on. It was usually bottles of IV saline solution, and I would grab a full box of twenty-four bottles and run to the surgical bunker. None of the doctors would look up, but one of the nurses would tell me the number they needed at that moment. Lt. J.G. Lynne was always calm but firm when giving orders, and she always said, "Thank you, Kinane." Nurse Lt. J.G. Martin was pretty much the same, but a little louder and much more firm. Her focus was hard to break, but when she did, you knew exactly what she wanted, and because of her polite nature, even under stress, she was also easy to work with. Most of the time, Nurse Lt. Cranfit would just bark at me and not use my name. I was just "CORPSMAN" to her, even though she was always poking her nose in my supply room and giving me a fake smile. I knew she was mean, and it seemed like she was always trying to show off for the surgeons, but mostly for CO Pitt. The other nurses and doctors would actually look up when she would order me around and speak to me like I was a dog. They always put their head back down to the patient they were working on and shook their heads. One time, I recall Lt. J.G. Martin said, "Easy on Kinane, Lieutenant. Kinane was called here, and he's only here to deliver what we need." That was the only time she was corrected by someone in front of me, and I understand she ripped Nurse Martin a new one that evening and gave her extra duty. CO Pitt mediated and overturned Cranflake's order for Martin to do extra work.

We did watch a lot of good movies, when evening time permitted. *Bonnie and Clyde* several times. *The Dirty Dozen* several times. *The Sand Pebbles*, *The Graduate*, but my personal favorite, and this film still is to this day, *In Like Flint*. I loved that film, and watched it every time it was shown in the chow hall. I've seen it at least a dozen times, and still watch some of it from time to time. The only difference now is that I can see how goofy it was. Now it makes me laugh.

The Marines stationed on base were primarily security: guarding the wire and front gate, and once or twice a week, gathering up a platoon-sized group, with a corpsman and interpreter, to go on a local search-and-destroy mission at night. Almost all were done at sunset, and that platoon would return the next morning—most times in good shape, and other times, carrying one or two of their own who were wounded or KIA. Marines felt a deep commitment to not leaving anyone behind, and they really meant it. Several times, interpreter Kim would be requested to go out with them because he was the easiest to understand and really seemed to hate the North Vietnamese, and Viet Cong. Marines liked him the way I liked him. He did his job quietly and didn't waste time. Kim was so brave, and always so willing to help Marines.

I didn't hang out with any of the Marines on base, but I would see them walking through the bunkers or past my supply room. They were whispering most of the time, or they were laughing about something. There were many days those same Marines would come back from a mission where one of their buddies had been KIA, and they were inconsolable for hours. Some crying quietly with other Marines, and never in front of Navy people like me. I always saw them from a distance. These rock-hard, battle-tested Marines were human, and any loss was important to the survivors. Those nights were emotional, and really the only time corpsmen engaged face-to-face with Marines. Our instructions from Pitt on those days was to listen to them. Listen for as long as they needed someone to listen. That's what Izzy and Branch and I did several nights. The Marines were experiencing the kind of pain that leaves an invisible scar. Our jobs were to get them through a brief period of time realizing their loss and what had happened out in the bush. The mourning never seemed to last more than twenty-four hours on base, because everyone was needed for the next group of casualties who were sure to come at any time, day or night, and sometimes multiple times a day. Charlie Med certainly was a busy base, I thought.

On November 20, 1967, CO Pitt was trying to assign a corpsman to a platoon going out at sunset. None of the E-1 to E-3 corpsmen were available, and three Navy corpsmen were actually KIA with Marines at Khe Sanh fire base. We were down to only four non-NCO corpsmen. Several had demobilized, because their year was up or they had become casualties themselves, and were removed from the war zone. Branch was really short and was going home right after Thanksgiving that Thursday, November 23rd. CO Pitt didn't want him to go out, and Izzy had already been out with platoons on three separate occasions. CO Pitt came to the supply room and said, "Hey, listen, Kinane. I told you I didn't think you would ever be asked to go out in the bush with a Marine platoon, but I think I'm going to need you to saddle up and muster at the base LZ at 1800 tonight."

What he had just said literally stopped me in my tracks. I looked at him, with my lower jaw on my chest, and slowly said, "Yes, sir."

He continued. "I really don't want you to go, and I definitely don't want you to get hurt out there, but each platoon needs one corpsman and one interpreter. I'll be sending your buddy Kim out with you, if I send you. Chances are very strong you'll be out there under the stars tonight, and it looks like it's going to really rain again. I want you to get yourself ready, relax, and hope I can find someone other than you to send out. I've already tried, but I think you'll be going." He left my supply room telling me, "Relax, you'll survive, Kinane."

I just stood there and started to pray quietly to myself and think about finding my field med pack so that I could make sure it was ready too. I realized in that moment, I had not even picked up a weapon since arriving over two months ago. I was not comfortable, and the adrenaline was flowing rapidly through my system. I wasn't afraid as much as I was actually intrigued and excited about what was happening and what would happen out there.

I found out later that Lt. Cranflake had recommended that I go out in the bush with a platoon on several occasions, and apparently this time, she swayed the CO with the suggestion that I go out. When I did confirm this, I sensed she was somehow trying to get rid of me. I was angry thinking about that for quite some time. Based on what I knew about Pitt, he would not have considered me without someone in his ear convincing him I should earn my corpsman grade in the field. It was at about that time I started thinking she was trying to get rid of me for some reason. If she only knew how much I wanted to get out of there, and back home, she might have approached things differently. Why she was such an asshole I didn't think I would ever understand. I found out how time would find a way to shed some light on Lt. Cranflake.

Sunset was at 1730 that evening, and I was one of the first troops out to muster on the LZ. That's where I met Marine Staff Sergeant Haug. He was from Minnesota and had been in the Marines for over ten years. We greeted each other, and while he was looking at the gear I was packing, he said, "We've heard a lot of good things about you, Kinane, and I don't want you to worry or freak out while we're out there."

I was listening to him with every fiber of my being. "Understood, Sergeant."

He seemed hardened, and he didn't display much emotion while talking to me. "You do everything I tell you, and you stay within four meters of my position this entire mission. Is that understood?"

I said, "Absolutely, Sergeant." He knew I was scared shitless, even though I tried so hard not to be overly concerned. I couldn't hide anything from this soldier. After Sergeant Haug checked my gear, Sergeant Perez walked up to us and looked right at me. He said, "Kinane, I hear Lt. Cranflake suggested you go out with us tonight. Believe me, Kinane, I don't agree with her on this, and she's a bitch." He repeated what Staff Sergeant Haug had just told me about staying close to them.

I knew I was actually trembling, but I was trying to control it so none of the other Marines or interpreter Kim would see my fear. As we got together for that muster, Sergeant Perez called out all sixteen names in the platoon for this search-and-destroy mission. After the head-count, he said, "Our interpreter will be handling the radio on this mission, and we want to welcome Corpsman Kinane, because this is his first mission outside the wire tonight. He's a really good corpsman, and he's told me he's ready for this job."

All the Marines responded with some kind of grunt in the affirmative, and then we started walking outside the gate in two single lines, separated by three or four yards from the Marine in front. We kept a separation in the event of a sniper attack, land mine, or booby trap. Staff Sergeant told everyone to stay quiet, and that he would stop every 200 yards to reestablish a "fallback" area. As we left, his final words were "Stay alert, and know every inch of where you are stepping."

I thought to myself, *Watch your feet, Kinane*. That's what all those signs were really talking about. Watch your feet indeed. Of course, nobody kept looking down the entire hump, but in addition to paying attention to the landscape and everything in the dense bush we were entering, we were always looking at our steps five feet before we got there.

Staff Sergeant Haug and Sergeant Perez were amazing from the first steps outside the wire. Haug told me to march in front of him, and he was at the rear of the platoon. Perez was near point. His platoon knew him, and knew how he moved outside the wire. The pace was slow, and we stopped every time Perez or Haug gave a fist above their shoulders.

We stopped often. He said this for my benefit the first three or four times: "This is our new fallback, understand, Kinane?"

It all made sense. If either Perez or Haug needed to yell "FALL BACK," we knew where to fall back to. After about the second mile or third "klick," as in kilometer, we would establish a new fallback position. The platoon had made this hump several times, and the point Marine, who was so brave and exposed to ambush, knew the path for this mission. These were seasoned Marines, and all had seen combat action. As I thought about that, I wondered if I would be eligible for a Combat Medical Badge (CMB) after this. Was an actual firefight required, or was it given just for going out? I found out later, and it wasn't that important to me while I was in-country, but it seemed like an honorable medal to have. It showed some level of courage in my mind. As I recall, every Marine on base had already received their Combat Action Badge (CAB) way before that night's mission.

We stopped the first time around 2100 and rested for fifteen minutes. We stopped again around 0100 (11/21) and ate C-rations. When you're really hungry, most of the food in the C-ration box is okay; not great, but not bad. We stopped one more time at 0400. These were rest breaks, and at the last break, several Marines asked me for some of the extra water in one of my three canteens. I was happy to give them a big sip, and they thanked me. As we humped back toward the base around 0500, everyone was really tired. Perez and Haug kept saying, "Stay alert, stay alert!" They knew darn well we were all tired, and I'm sure they were too.

When we were near the edge of the jungle, a low-flying plane swooped right above the entire platoon. Haug and Perez yelled, "Double time, double time!" We all started jogging toward the edge of the jungle, not far from the front gate of the base, but we were sprayed with Agent Orange—drenched. It was white coming down, and it smelled like weed killer. I knew the protocol for being sprayed was to hose off at the base as soon as possible. We were sweating, and now this shit was getting into our eyes and mouths. Everyone was coughing and spitting while running to the open area just outside the jungle. Haug sent a message on the radio to stop the aerial herbicide spraying until we got back in less than thirty minutes. The spraying stopped, and the low-flying C-123 Provider flew away and towards the east. We gathered, and everyone took out a towel or handkerchief from their pockets and started wiping their faces. Coughing and spitting for a few minutes, prior to heading towards the base, which we could see about a mile away, I told Haug and Perez, "Everyone will need to head straight for the hose and be hosed off when get back on base."

They said, "We know. We understand, Kinane."

I was sweating profusely and wiping around my eyes when it happened. I was partially blinded, but we were so close to the gate, I was simply moving forward as quickly as I could, and yelling out, "GET HOSED DOWN! GET HOSED DOWN!" While double-timing it, I felt an incredible pain in my lower back. My upper outer gluteus maximus, I thought. Serious PAIN! I lunged forward about seven feet, falling to the ground with a yelp, while looking back. In that spit second, I thought I had been shot, and thought it was a sniper behind me. Just as I was on the ground looking back, I realized a Vietnamese soldier, or some Viet Cong, had been hiding in a spider hole and came out of it as I passed. This dude had stabbed me in the left ass cheek with his, are you kidding me, FUCKING bayonet! He put a three-inch gash into my left butt cheek, and thankfully his bayonet only penetrated about an inch. He was charging toward me with his bayonet, yelling, and about to give me another stab as a kind of coup de grace, but just as I saw him charging towards me, Staff Sergeant Haug opened fire on the dude. Haug's rounds hit him from the belt line up, hitting his torso and his face. He immediately collapsed in half, falling away from me on the ground. Perez walked over to the dude and shot three more rounds into him because he said he was still breathing and talking. He was upset, and he put him out of his misery, saying he still had his hand on his weapon. After those three rounds, he was dead. Haug and Perez both agreed he was hard-core North Vietnamese Regular Army (NVA).

The other Marines had set up a small perimeter around me, and Perez grabbed my med pack and pulled out some large bandages and tape. I got to my feet, but I was bleeding through my pants, and the blood was running down my leg, into my left boot. Perez cut my pants at the site of the wound and said, "Goddamn, Kinane, he got you good. You'll survive."

I said, "Thank you. I'll take care of this," as I pressed down on the wound and starting limping towards the base.

Haug said, "You'll get a Purple Heart for this, Kinane. The enemy shed your blood." He went on to give me shit about not paying attention to the ground, and how didn't I see that fucking spider hole.

I said, "Spider hole?"

Perez said, "Yeah, he came out of that spider hole and went after you. You've got to watch out for that, Kinane."

As we were about to enter the gate of the base, Haug and Perez concluded that this may have been the sniper they knew was nearby, outside the wire. They said something about trying to find that sniper for weeks. He must have been really hungry, and knew what he was doing was suicide. I just listened and pressed the gauze on my upper outer gluteus maximus.

At the gate, my gear was taken off my back, and I was put on a stretcher. They took me to the hose and sprayed me down while I was on the stretcher and ran me into the main medical tent and into surgery. All the Marines who were doused with that Agent Orange were spraying themselves off, clothes and all. They were swearing and laughing. I was happy they were doing that, because that shit was bad to be exposed to.

The first people I saw as I was transferred to a surgical table were nurses Lt. J.G. Lynne and Lt. J.G. Martin. They had heard on the radio I had been wounded, and started working on my wound quickly. They took my shirt off and cut off my pants after removing my boots. They were so fast. They set me up on an IV and gave me a shot of morphine, which was the first time I had ever needed morphine, but it helped with the pain within twenty seconds after injection. They were actually joking with me, telling me I would be fine, and just then CO Pitt arrived with XO Granato. XO Granato took over, while Pitt called me a hero and chuckled that I was okay and left. XO Granato stitched me up quickly and stopped the bleeding. I recall Dr. Granato asking me to give him my battery commander so he could recommend a field promotion. I think I laughed. I was already so tired from the night hump, and now the morphine was kicking in, so I just fell asleep right on that table.

I woke up later that afternoon in the recovery bunker. I was in there with only one other Marine, and I could hear a helicopter landing on the base; he was being transported to the ship and off the base. I thought I would be transferred too, but Lt. Cranflake came up to me and said, "You're not leaving the base, Kinane. You'll be recovering from your wound here, and you should be back to regular duty in a couple days. CO Pitt will make that call for you." As she left, she said, "You're lucky, Kinane, and you'll get better." For some reason, she didn't seem sincere telling me that, and frankly, I recall thinking she was upset about something as she walked away out of the bunker, towards the chow hall and main medical bunker.

That night Pitt, Haug, and Perez came up to my recovery bed and talked to me about what had happened. They were genuinely happy I would recover quickly, and said it was a million-dollar wound, which I really didn't understand, but I chuckled quietly with them. Pitt told me that I would be getting a Purple Heart within the next couple weeks. The paperwork needed to go through. I thanked Haug and Perez, and they told me to get well ASAP as they left the recovery bunker. CO Pitt said he was happy I was okay, and then asked me if I had taken any time off. I told him I had not since joining because I didn't like downtime and never felt I really needed time off. He reminded me that I had many days of vacation available and that he wanted me to take some R&R for at least a few days. I said, "Yes, sir." He asked me where I wanted to go, because he could get me anywhere in country, even to Thailand or the Philippines for a few days. He reminded me that he really needed me to do my main job, and that it would seem like a stretch for him to put me on another mission like the other night. I told him how much I learned, and how much I appreciated what our Marines did out on a hump in the bush. He agreed and said, "Do you want to take a few days off down south in Saigon?"

I thought about that and said, "Yes, sir, I would enjoy that."

"Fine, you rest, and I'll try to get you on a chopper to Saigon sometime tomorrow. You should be able to walk, and the time off will be good for you. Anyway, it's better than just sitting around here."

I said, "Yes, sir, thank you."

He said he would arrange everything and told me that the movie that night was *The Dirty Dozen*. "It's the base premier of the film. I hope you can make it, Kinane. We'll have you in a wheelchair, unless you can hobble there without breaking your ass stiches," he said, laughing a little.

I said, "Thank you, sir. I will hobble there for chow and wait for the film."

"Good, glad you'll be okay, and believe me, Kinane, you got lucky, but you'll be okay." He turned around and walked out towards the chow hall and main medical bunker.

I was surprised because interpreter Kim kept me company while I was on the rack in the recovery bunker. He told me that he was about ten meters behind me when the NVA jumped out of the spider hole and attacked me. He saw the entire thing and said I was very lucky to be alive. I agreed. We really got to know each other, and he was a great guy. He told me his dream was to live in America. He had lost his entire family a few years before, and he felt he was on the right path to become an American citizen, pursue his medical degree, and become a doctor. I was really impressed with him. There was a sadness about him, and he would often become quiet and meditative. He tried to teach me some words I would need on my R&R to Saigon, and made a suggestion about where to eat and where not to go while I was there. He said he had been to Saigon many times, and that's where he was hired by the U.S. Military as an interpreter. He was thirty-one years old, thin, and probably five and half feet tall. Very strong. Incredibly strong hands. His hands were already very rough. He told me he had worked in many rice fields and chopped down a lot of trees. His smile was genuine, and when he laughed, he laughed quietly, but he liked to laugh, that was for sure. He was always at the chow hall at night watching movies and always sat in the back. I really appreciated him keeping me company when I was awake on that rack recovering from the freakin' bayonet wound.

That night, November 23, was Thanksgiving, and the Marine cooks prepared a great meal, which included turkey, stuffing, mashed potatoes, gravy, and green beans. During dinner, everyone was very nice to me, and they were rooting for me. Some would joke about getting it in the ass, but it seemed everyone on base knew who I was. I thought I was invisible for the first two months, but it was that evening, I realized how much Marines care about people, and especially corpsmen. The only one who didn't say anything or smile at me was Cranflake. I noted a scowl on her face and passed it off, as she was always grumpy. She was just angry at the world for some reason, and she liked to take it out on others, especially anyone below her rank.

The film was great, and the room was packed. After the film, I went back to see Di Di Mau near my bed, and I saw Izzy and Branch. They said they had been taking care of her for me, and that she was a great little dog. I was so glad to see her and know that others cared for her too. Those two hooch mates were so cool, and happy to see me too. I told them I had to spend the night in the recovery bunker, and that I was headed on three-day R&R to Saigon the next day. I told them Pitt had insisted, and it sounded cool to me. They said they would make sure Di Di Mau was fed and taken care of while I was gone. I was so grateful, and I headed towards the recovery bunker in my wheelchair. I slept well that night.

Day two of my stay in recovery bunker was my last day in there. I was able to go back to my rack and footlocker to get a change of clothes. I was told to hold off on showering for a few days, so I sponged as much of my body down as I could. I shaved and brushed my teeth. After noon chow, Pitt came over to me and said, "A chopper is on the way to take you down to Saigon. I need you to take this package to the TOC at Tan Son Nhut Air Base, just outside Saigon, and check in there for your brief visit to Saigon." They would shuttle me back and forth to the downtown area of Saigon, where

American soldiers were relatively safe. He said I should grab a beer and whispered into my ear, "Get laid, Kinane."

I laughed. "Roger that, sir."

The chopper touched down at our base around 1400, and the crew said, "Welcome, Doc." I wondered how they knew I was a corpsman, but I figured Pitt had told them.

I replied, "Hi, guys! Thanks for the ride," and we were on our way south.

We arrived at Tan Son Nhut Air Base just before 1600, and I was pointed where to go to check in and get assigned a temporary rack. I was shown where I would be sleeping for the next couple of nights, and then I had chow. This was a much bigger chow hall, and the food was good. I went to the movie theater bunker, and they were also showing *Dirty Dozen* that night. I was happy to watch it again. I remember being amazed to see Jim Brown in a film. He was such a great football player, and I couldn't take my eyes off him every time he was in the picture. I really enjoyed that film, and decided to hit my rack and head out to downtown, the American-friendly area of Saigon.

I rolled out of my temporary rack around 6 a.m. and S.S.S. before hitting breakfast chow. That chow hall was packed, and seemed to feed ten times more troops than Charlie Med. I noted many officers, and especially many Special Forces, with their cavalry black hats. Everything was fascinating to me that day. People were talking quietly in groups at long tables and occasionally laughing out loud. Outside this large chow hall structure, which might have been an airplane hangar before it was a chow hall, you could hear planes flying over. Jets were landing or taking off, and they were incredibly loud. It was clearly an Air Force base, because of the number of soldiers in their Air Force uniform of the day. I enjoyed my eggs, bacon, and potatoes that morning, and asked a guy eating near me where the shuttle was to go to Saigon. He explained that it was right outside the Post Exchange (PX), just outside the front of the chow hall, and pointed to where the front was. I thanked him and headed that direction. I wanted to see as much of Saigon as I could and find a place for a cold beer. I had become aware through scuttlebutt on base that there were bars like Chicago Bar, New York Bar, Texas Bar, or Philadelphia Bar. Each bar tried to cater to a certain segment of U.S. soldiers, but you didn't have to be from that town to get in. I was wondering what kind of beer the Chicago bar had. I had been craving an Old Style or even a Hamm's for months.

The shuttle bus was half full with about ten troops in the same green casual uniform with a soft green cap, and the ride from Tan Son Nhut to Saigon was about twenty-five minutes. I recognized one of the Marines from Charlie Med. He was on the bus and nodded to me with a smile. "Hey, Kinane," he said.

I said, "Hey, buddy, good to see you."

The driver asked everyone to listen up because he wanted to give us crucial information. A Marine sergeant, he continuously gave us information about the main street, Nguyen Hue Street, in the district that was safe for Americans. He had a Military Police (MP) armband on and told us to be careful and not get too drunk. He said soldiers had been mugged, knifed, and even killed while in Saigon for a day of R&R. He gave us the shuttle schedule, and where he was dropping us off would be the same place to bring us back to the base. He said the last ride was 2300 and not to miss that bus back. Absence Without Leave (AWOL) or Unauthorized Absence (UA) charges would be tagged to our records if we missed that last bus. Getting back before 0900 the next day was the only choice, unless MPs picked us up.

The last five minutes of the ride, we were actually driving in Saigon, and it was fascinating. The MP driver started joking with us, telling us where his favorite places were. He told us about food, beer, hookers. He actually had a small box of condoms at the front of the bus and encouraged all of us to grab a couple on Uncle Sam. He pulled up to a stop where two soldiers were waiting on a bench. He told us all to have a good time, and be careful. Viet Cong were everywhere. We exited the bus and started checking out this main street.

I was the last to leave the bus, because I wanted to confirm the time and location for the final shuttle back to Tan Son Nhut Air Base. He said, "I'm glad you asked," and repeated what he had said earlier. I said thanks, and before I stepped off the bus, I asked for a couple of those condoms. The driver smiled, and said "Have fun, but don't spend any more than $30 bucks on a lady." I nodded, and laugh, as I stepped off the bus. I looked around at that corner for about ten minutes, trying to check out everything. There were hundreds of people, mostly Vietnamese, walking around, riding motorcycles, and driving older small cars. That day was cloudy, but dry and warm. I remember noticing all the great food smells, and hearing chickens or roosters making their noises all over. As

I was able to focus, I could see food vendors all up and down both sides of this big street. The buildings all had apartments or offices above some restaurant, gift shop, or clothing store. I wanted to check out everything.

And then I spotted it—less than a half block away. "Chicago Bar - .25 cent draft, Old Style, Hamm's, Schlitz, and Budweiser." Someone had also painted a flag of Chicago above the door. I started walking right toward the bar, and while passing other joints, someone was telling me to come in there or buy this or that. They were aggressive salespeople for sure. All I could do was look at the name of the bar, the beers, and the price. I kept thinking how good this first cold beer would taste after so many months. Before I walked into the bar, I noticed another bar right next door, the Philadelphia Bar, and they were also advertising "live poker" games.

As I stepped into the Chicago Bar, I noticed a Vietnamese stripper on the stage in the far corner, out of the corner of my eye, as I headed straight to the bar. It smelled of musty old beer and some kind of "Mr. Clean" smell. Some of the chairs remained upside down on most of the tables, but there were several open tables in front of the stage. It was dark, like any typical old tavern in Chicago. The floor was an old and per-manently stained dirty wood. I noticed two other guys at the end of the bar, secretly talking as they noticed me walk in. I grabbed a stool at the bar and put out a five-dollar bill and asked for a cold draft of Old Style. The bartender was an old-er woman, and she smiled and said, "Yes, right away." She walked towards the fridge, pulled out a big cold mug, and poured my Old Style in front of me. She placed my beer on a coaster, which had the logo of the Chicago Bears. I thought that was so cool. She made change of my five dollars, and returned four dollars and three quarters. I gave her one of the dollars, and she was thrilled and said, "Thanks, honey," and walked towards those guys at the end of the bar. I immediately took a big gulp of that ice-cold beer. It brought me right back to the Wrigley Field bleachers with my vendor friend, Richard, and I wondered what he was doing. I hoped he was still in school on his way to a law degree.

I could hear the music in the room that the stripper was dancing to. It was "Satisfaction" by the Rolling Stones. I really enjoyed hearing that at that very moment, and started to pull the frosty mug to my mouth when I was tapped on my shoulder. It was that Marine from Charlie Med who was on the bus into town. He was with three other Marines, and they were laughing at me and the stripper on the stage. His last name was Brock, according to his green shirt. He said, "What the fuck are you DOING in here, Kinane?"

I was surprised he knew my name, but I said, "I'm here for this awesome twenty-five-cent mug of Chicago beer."

"You sure you're not here for the stage show, Kinane?"

I said, "I barely noticed. I wanted to drink this beer for months."

Marine Brock took a step back, nodded at me, and chuckled. He told his buddies to go with him to a table in front of the stage, and I watched them all go to the front table, not three feet away from the stripper. I wasn't wearing my glasses, and it was dark, so I figured they wanted a "titty show." They were sitting there laughing as I gulped down my first cold mug of beer. I had just ordered a second mug when Brock stood up right next to the stage with what looked like a dollar bill in his hand, ready to put it in the stripper's G-string. As the stripper wiggled up to him, Brock clearly dwarfed the stripper, who was Vietnamese. Brock grabbed the G-string as the two guys at the end of the bar started towards him at the stage. The stripper and the two Vietnamese guys walking towards the stage started yelling, telling Brock to let him go and to get the hell out. One of the guys yelled back to the bartender to call MPs. Before they got to him, Brock yelled at me through the bar for everyone to hear. The stripper kid was trying to pull Brock's hand off his crotch, and Brock stumbled away from the stage, laughing with the other Marines he was with. He was leaving, and pointing at me. "See, Kinane! See what you made me do!"

It really was funny when I think about it, but I certainly didn't want to get locked up on my first day of R&R. While Brock was laughing with his buddies, he said, "Kinane! We see swinging dicks every day, and because this joint is selling beer for a quarter, you don't realize it's a fag bar? That's too much, Kinane!"

I didn't realize that the stripper on stage was a dude. I really was there ONLY for that Chicago draft beer. Brock and his buddies got up and followed me out the door. I left a dollar on the bar and never took another sip of beer there. It just wasn't my kind of joint. Love the beer, but there were bars all over on this street. As I tumbled out of the Chicago Bar, I laughed to myself and said, "Swinging dicks?" I hadn't heard that since basic. It was so funny, but I realized I had to begin paying very close attention to where I was going. I'll never forget that moment.

I started walking down the street. I wasn't hungry, but the food smelled good. As I was walking away, I could see Brock and his buddies being tossed out of the bar, and tossing a punch at one of those two guys. They were laughing and fighting at the same time, and Brock said, "See you back at Charlie Med, Kinane!"

I waved back at him, and got some distance from all the Marines doing what they do best. Fighting. I was looking at all the shops and saying "No thanks" to all the people trying to get me into their shop or bar. I found a small restaurant and bought two egg rolls, and they were excellent, with this really tasty dipping sauce. I started thinking about that Philadelphia Bar and the live poker, so I started walking back towards that place. It smelled like Philly steak sandwiches, and that smell brought me back to Burger Ville in Chicago. As I passed the Chicago Bar, I took a peek inside and noticed my cold mug of beer still on the bar. I decided right away to chalk that beautiful mug of beer up, and leave it there. As I got to the front of the Philadelphia Bar, an older lady with a cigar in her mouth said, "You play poker, GI?" I stopped, smiled at her, and tried to scope out the inside of the bar. I wanted to make sure it wasn't a strip club, so I could avoid uncomfortable situations, and I wasn't sure if Brock was spying on me or not. The bar didn't have a stage that I could see, and the music was Vietnamese. Not rock & roll. I noticed several tables with dealers. It was 11:00 in the morning, and three of the poker tables were full with six or seven players at each table. Everyone playing was Vietnamese, but they seemed friendly and genuinely happy to have me possibly join the table they were sitting at. I immediately thought, *They think I'm some kind of chump.* I nodded, and smiled, while taking some time to absorb the room.

I walked over to the bar and ordered a draft Budweiser. That mug was almost as good as the Old Style. I brought my beer over to the tables, where they were all playing "No Limit Texas Hold'em" poker. A game I enjoyed and knew how to play. Each table had a dealer. I had never seen this before. I had played a lot of poker while I was in high school, but only for nickels and dimes. This was far more serious. I had saved all my pay up until that day. I was being paid almost $200 per month for the last several months since getting my crow, and I had just over $100 dollars in my pocket. I didn't want to lose it, but I felt comfortable sitting down and getting into one of these games. The moment I sat down, in between hands, the dealer motioned for people to come to the table and simply pointed at me. As he was pointing, I was grabbing my bills from my pocket. The first young Vietnamese lady asked me how many chips I wanted to start with, and that a rack of chips would be $50. As I was settling in, the game stopped as the dealer shuffled the cards. Everyone at the table made me feel welcome, and they were all smoking cigars or cigarettes. There were four older guys and one guy much younger. I figured he was in his mid-twenties, but I was always terrible at judging ages, so he could have been fifty years old. I really wasn't sure, but for some reason, I wanted to keep an eye on him. All the other guys seemed peaceful and only wanted to play cards.

The second person, another young lady, walked up to me and saw my mug of beer on the coaster on the table, and she said, "Let me know when you want another drink."

I said, "Thank you!" I ended up playing poker for five hours straight. I didn't even get up to hit the head. I was worried my money on the table would disappear, as I was winning and my stack of chips started getting some attention. I wasn't sure how much I was up, but I knew I had more than doubled my initial $50 around 1400. The cards were just coming. Not every hand, but many, and I was playing very tight much to the disappointment of the guys at the table. They wanted to win their money back, and I didn't want that to happen. I finally got hungry and said, "I'm done, fellas." They all let out a groan and tried to dissuade me from cashing in. I told them I was really hungry and had to get back to the bus stop so I could get back to the base. They knew the last bus didn't leave for hours, and knew I was cutting out while I was ahead with their cash. I grabbed all my chips and went to the cashier at the back of the bar. I put five trays of chips on the counter, and the Vietnamese guy, who I think was the bar owner, started counting out American dollars. I had won over $800, and I could not believe how lucky I was. The beers were good, but I certainly wasn't drunk. I had to piss badly, so I hit the head before I left. I recall feeling really good as I left that bar. I had never had that much money, ever. The smile on my face as I walked in circles in front was obvious, I'm sure.

I was close to the bus stop and started walking towards it, even though I still had a few hours to kill if I wanted. I thought about food on the base and simply getting back before dark. Just as I was thinking that, I caught a young woman out of the corner of my eye. She was waving at me, asking me to come over. She was standing in front of another bar and smiling at me. She had a white short dress on and dark hair piled on top of her head, like Elizabeth Taylor. She looked very beautiful, and seemed to be in her twenties. She was a little over five feet tall with her heels and was wearing a nice dress. Her make-up was nice, and she had nice black hair in curls. She looked great, and I had to stop and think for a couple of minutes. I was across the street from where she was, so I just looked around trying to make a decision about going over there and missing evening chow on base so I could hang out with her a while. I decided I would get on the next bus and buy some geedunk and maybe even jump on the last bus back to base at 2300. I told myself, *Do NOT miss that last bus, especially with all this cash in your pocket. Don't be a fool, Charlie. Be careful.* She was smiling and waving to other guys as I walked across the street, dodging motorcycles, before she realized I was coming over to her.

I introduced myself, and she asked me to come in and have a drink with her. Apparently, that was one of her jobs, so she could hustle at that bar. She grabbed my arm and asked me my name. I said, "Charlie, and yours?"

She said, "Call me Stella tonight. Do you know what Stella means in Italian?" She answered her own question quickly, but before she did, I could only think of Marlon Brando in that film. She said "Stella means Star."

I chuckled while wondering what her name was the day before, and said, "Nice to meet you, Stella." We walked over to the bar, and sat down on a stool.

Stella said, "Some people call me by my middle name, Merced."

I said, "Really," as if it mattered in my mind. The lady bartender walked over to us, smiled, and said, "What will you have?"

I said, "Whatever she's having, and a cold draft mug of beer for me."

Stella immediately started complimenting me, telling me she liked my hair and my eyes. She stood up and took a good look at my entire body and said, "You look strong."

I said, "Thank you, Stella."

The bartender served a beer in front of me and what looked like a small glass of Coke for Stella. She said, "Seventy-five cents for your beer, and five dollars for her drink."

I stopped and looked at the bartender, until I figured out the little game Stella was playing. I laughed and said, "Okay," and handed her seven dollar bills, while turning slightly away from Stella so she couldn't see the wad of cash I had. I realized at that moment, she was a real Vietnamese hooker. The suggested words of CO Pitt rang in my head a few times. "Get laid, Kinane." I laughed and said to myself be careful, but see what happens. She was so pretty, and she spoke very nice English, with a slight French accent. Her smile was bright, and her teeth were clean. She had heavy lipstick on, and after I paid, she gave me a little peck of a kiss on my right cheek. After the little kiss, she seemed to be thinking about something. I just smiled at her, while smelling her heavy perfume. She actually seemed nervous as she said, "You want to get a room, Charlie?"

I said, "Let's see what happens after this beer, Stella." She smiled and turned away briefly. She was nervous. I wondered why, and her being nervous started to make me feel nervous too.

After I finished my first beer, I decided to ask her a few questions. "Where can we go?"

She smiled, looked around, and waved her right arm up, as if to signal somebody in the back of the bar. She said, "I'll have a room upstairs for us in ten minutes."

My eyes got wide open, and I nodded and said, "All right."

She leaned into me and kissed me on my ear and face. She started rubbing her body on mine and said, "Thirty dollars for one hour, and anything you want." I smiled and looked down at her hand, exposing one of her breasts secretly for my eyes only. That convinced me she was a woman. She quickly put her breast back under her clothes and asked me, "Twenty dollars for only blow job."

I said, "I should be okay with thirty dollars."

She smiled and said, "Buy me one more drink, and then we will go."

I wondered about that request, but I figured that was some house rule for these ladies. I sighed, thought about it for five seconds, thought about my winnings, and said, "Sure, why not."

She waved for the bartender, and the lady brought over another Coke for her and asked me if I wanted another beer. I said, "No, thank you. I've had enough." She smiled and asked me for five dollars. I gave her the bill. Stella guzzled her glass of Coke, which was about four ounces, and grabbed my hand, leading me towards the hallway stairs in the back of the room. There was an older Vietnamese guy at the bottom of the stairs who asked me for five dollars. He said it was for the room. Again, I thought about that for about five seconds and secretly pulled another five out of my pocket and handed it over. He said, "Up the stairs, second door on the left." Stella started up the stairs in front of me, teasing me with her dress by pulling it up to show me her butt. She was laughing and teasing me. Turning around and giving me the "Come here" finger, and sticking her tongue out at me in the sexiest way. It wasn't dirty. It was sensual and sexy. I had a chub from the first step up those stairs, and this wasn't going away. We got to the top of the stairs and went left to the second door. She knocked and smiled at me. She opened the door and said, "Come in, Charlie," while removing her dress three seconds after I closed the door.

She grabbed me by my shirt and started unbuttoning it, one button at a time. She said, "You think I'm beautiful?"

I watched her hands and said, "Yes, Stella, you're very beautiful."

She said, "I like you, Charlie," and started kissing me on my mouth, twisting her tongue on mine. It seemed like she was trying to slurp up my entire face. She seemed genuinely excited and into it too, even though I kept wondering how much of this was a regular act. She stopped kissing me and pulled away from me, about two feet. She was taking off her black bra and black panties that matched her beautiful hair. I couldn't tell how old she was, but I knew she was more than three times seven, and maybe even close to thirty. She was standing there showing me her front, with her hands over her breasts, and turning around to show me her back side. She was so pretty. She slowly walked over to the bed and told me to take off my clothes. As I started to take off my shirt, she said, "Money first, please."

I said, "Oh yeah, of course," and pulled out three ten-dollar bills. She reached out her hand, blew me a kiss, and said, "You know, if you like this, tips are much appreciated."

I said, "Sounds good to me," thinking that those guys at that poker table were paying for this, so cool. She watched as I got naked and got up from the bed and she suggested a bath and massage for an extra ten bucks. I looked at the old tub in the room and several clean white towels, and said, "Sure, why not. As long as I don't get these stitches wet." She asked for the extra ten, and I gave it to her. She walked over to the tub, put the plug in the bottom, and started filling it with water as she tested the temperature of the water with her hand. Then she got in and invited me in with her. She told me to sit on the edge of the tub so I could keep my wound dry. I couldn't hide my erection from her, and she was looking at it as I got only my lower legs into the tub. As the tub filled she put soap on a wash cloth and started to wash every inch of my body. She paid close attention to my throbbing erection, occasionally pleasing me orally and stroking me with her hand as her other hand washed me down. I had to move her hand away as I felt like I was about to come, and I didn't want to ruin this moment. I fondled her breasts and felt her body with both hands as she washed me with some nice-smelling soap. We kissed, and she moaned.

After about ten minutes, she pulled the plug and got up while the water drained. She handed me a towel and started to towel her body off in front of me. I couldn't take my eyes off her. I remember being happy about not getting my stitches wet. She dropped her towel and told me her name was really Anne. I said, "Not Stella or Merced?"

She said, "No, Anne. If I don't like a guy, I never tell them my real name." She kissed me, and somehow, like a magic trick that happens so fast, she had a condom on me, pulled me into bed, and said, "I like you, Charlie."

The sex didn't last too long, but I recall it was amazing. She brought me to orgasm twice within that one hour. I was more than satisfied. She told me to come back to her soon, and we walked down the stairs, where she walked me to the front of the bar, kissed me, and said, "See you next time, Charlie." It was only 1930, and the bus stop was only a half block away. I started walking, thinking, *I just got laid, and I have tons of money in my pocket.* The body vibrations from the sex with Anne, or Stella, or Merced, whatever her name, were good vibrations. I was able to get on the 2100 bus back to Tan Son Nhut Air Base. What an amazing day. I never got to Saigon again, but I'll never forget that day.

I returned to Charlie Med the following Monday, and the first thing I noticed was that the supply room was a mess again. I couldn't believe it. Pitt had asked Lt. Cranfit to take over my job until I came back, and he was the only person to reconcile the control med audit I had established several weeks earlier. I could tell the command was busy because the recovery bunker, where I was a week before, was full of

126

soldiers recovering and/or stabilizing before being demobi-lized (d-mob). Pitt had come to the supply room to let me know what happened while I was gone, and said he would talk to Lt. Cranfit later about the mess. I said, "Thank you, sir. It's good to be back."

He said, "I hear you really had a good time. You should have stayed the extra day. Why didn't you?"

I said, "Sir, I just want to do my job here the best I can, and I am so grateful to you for trusting me with this job here at Charlie Med."

He nodded. "I'll catch you later. Make sure you replenish all supplies in the surgical bunker, and recovery bunker."

I said, "Aye, aye, sir."

It took me a couple hours to get the room back in order, and back to my regular job day to day. I was able to spend some time with Di Di Mau, Corpsman Branch, and Corpsman Izzy. They were so cool to take care of Di Di Mau, and they liked her too. I realized after coming back that everyone knew my last name, and most seemed to know Di Di Mau too. She became the unofficial Charlie Med mascot. I had written home to some family and friends about her, and even sent a picture. I knew I had many months to figure out the logistics to get her back home, so I made a note in my notebook calendar to start the process sometime early summer, before my one-year deployment here ended August of next year, 1968.

December 1967 went by quickly, as it seemed each day we got busier. Heavy enemy attacks were happening more regularly and with far more casualties almost every day. I saw so many soldiers horribly wounded and in pain. I always did everything I could on the staging area for their pain and wounds. It never seemed like enough, but so many of these Marines I was able to treat during that triage transition on base were so brave and dealt with their pain. They knew everyone around them was suffering, and as they had a brief moment of pain subsiding for themselves, they were trying to lift the spirits of the guys around them who were struggling, crying, screaming, and praying out loud. Each day, we saw bad things, and each day, I helped place KIA Marines in body bags to be sent home. Christmas was even busy. The enemy was relentless with their attacks and daily mortar and rocket fire on our base. The only time that was scary for me was when we were treating casualties on the outdoor staging area. The closest round came within ten yards, and we all prepared for the incoming.

Through December and into January, we could hear Rolling Thunder and Arc Light dropping thousands of big bombs up north. We were told they were bombing around the demilitarized zone (DMZ), which was just north of where the Marines were on Khe Sanh Combat Base (KSCB), north of us, and only a few klicks south of the DMZ. Those Marines were taking a beating, and they kept holding out. I couldn't imagine what they were dealing with. It was rough, and it was nasty. This was the beginning of the Battle of Khe Sanh, which lasted halfway into 1968.

I don't recall New Year's Day, but I do recall that Thursday, January 11, 1968. Charlie Med was under heavy mortar and rocket attack that entire day; each round hitting the base seemed closer to the bunkers than ever. It was easy to figure out how close they got by the sound of each explosion. The close rounds were loud and rattled the floors. One round hit right near the men's head/shower structure, and when they hit that loud, you knew it was close. It hit around 1700 when we were having evening chow, and several Marines got up from their meal to check out the damage and inspect the type of round that just came in. Marines always wanted to verify the enemy's weapons, so I knew they were doing an important job. So dangerous too, because they were taking a big risk by possibly being exposed to spent uranium fuel, if it was a rocket. I had finished my meal, and I was putting away my tray when one of the Marines came up to me and said, "We need you to see something, Kinane."

I said, "Sure," not really understanding why they needed me. I thought it had something to do with the supply room. Maybe it had taken some damage because of that close hit. I walked down the trench outside the chow hall bunker, and four Marines, Thompson, and Branch were standing in a circle with their heads down. As I got near them, they all looked at me at exactly the same time and said, "Di Di Mau is dead, Kinane. She took a direct hit apparently when she was doing her business out here." I felt devastated hearing those words. I went to look at her, and there was almost nothing left of her. All we could really make out was her one front paw, because that was her right front paw. The rest of her remains were gone, except some fur and some blood. She was basically obliterated. All I could say was "Motherfuckers!" I didn't want to sob, because I realized I had never sobbed over a KIA Marine, so out of respect for those Marines, I held back my tears as those wonderful Marines tried to cheer me up.

I said, "Would you guys help bury her with me?" I wanted to take her paw to the temporary cemetery area on base and bury her. I don't know why I did that, but I felt that was the thing to do, and they all agreed. We gave her a simple burial using a trench shovel. I put down a little rock for her marker. I've been sad about losing that little dog ever since. January 11, 1968 was a horrible day I will never forget.

The next day I will never forget was only a few weeks later. It was Monday, January 29, 1968. I had gotten the word again from CO Pitt that I was going out with a platoon at sunset again. I was still upset about losing Di Di Mau, and I had a bad frame of mind. I didn't care so much after that. I had become like a mechanical robot going through the regular base routine each day. I was noticeably quiet, and I think Pitt was trying to shake me loose from my despair. I know he still liked me, and I even know he was sad about losing Di Di Mau too. I think the entire base was, but human Marines were far more important for sure. Pitt's decision to put me back out with a platoon wasn't done in a mean way at all. Several of the E-3 corpsmen who would go out with platoons had been either KIA or wounded so badly that they were never coming back. Izzy was crucial in that surgical bunker with all the doctors, and Branch had already d-mob'd over a month before. He was out of the country and probably back home. We were all very happy for him, but losing him without an immediate replacement created stress on our manpower. We all worked very hard that January to make up for losses.

My wound from the bayonet was healing nicely, and I wasn't even limping anymore. On that day, I had no problem going back out on a search-and-destroy mission. Especially since Staff Sergeant Haug and Sergeant Perez had made a special request for me to be their corpsman that night. I actually felt a sense of honor, and I felt appreciated.

At 1730 that Monday night, we all gathered exactly where we had gathered on November 20th a couple of months ago. I couldn't believe Brock was on this mission too. He looked at me and smiled, but he definitely had a warrior's disposition this time. We went through all the same instructions, and before we lined up, Perez said a quick prayer out loud. We had not done that back in November, and I thought it was cool for some reason. When Perez was finished, and we all said, "Amen," Haug told us intel suggested very heavy enemy movement near the DMZ, and they were headed toward KSCB, on the border of Laos, which was only about thirty miles to our west. What he said got my attention, and I heard several of the Marines say, "Motherfuckers," as though they felt concerned for their own safety. Perhaps they were just cursing at the enemy in order to motivate themselves. Marines had a way of motivating themselves and the other Marines around them. Their verbal process is not for kids to hear because of the language they use, but believe me, they get motivated to kill, if given the chance.

Outside the main gate, I was walking right in front of Haug again, and I had a feeling we were going to see at least one firefight that night. I wasn't sure why I felt that way, but it just seemed like it. I double-checked my three canteens and my M-5 bag as we passed that spider hole and into the bush. It was getting darker earlier, so almost as soon as we hit the edge of the bush, the light from the sun was gone, and the darkness of the night descended upon our platoon as we marched quietly forward.

We made two stops during that night so we could rest a few minutes, drink a little water, and make sure we were all squared away. That's what I liked about Haug and Perez. They really cared about everyone. We made our third stop at 0100 and ate some C-rations. Just as we got up and started moving forward, we got hit.

From what I understand now, Brock was on point, and Perez was right behind him. Brock hit some trip wire, and the loudest explosion I had ever heard happened along with a big fireball. We had sixteen guys with us that night, and within a second, ten of them were down. We had all been hit by shrapnel. Thankfully, I was only grazed across the right cheek, under my eye. I was temporarily blinded, and I could hear small arms fire and screaming from everyone wounded and on the ground. I got hit twice. One time in the shoulder, and one time through my lower left leg. Haug was hit in the stomach right in front of me and he was trying to remove a big hot piece of shrapnel from just above his belt and below his flak jacket. He fell to the ground and pulled out the large metal piece from his abdomen. He was in trouble, but he soon started firing back towards where the enemy rounds fired, about thirty yards in the bush. All you could see was the fire coming out of the muzzles of the weapons they were firing at us.

Haug said, "Those are AK-47s, and it seems like one or two Browning automatic rifles." He could tell by the sound. Tracers were also coming from the enemy's position, and

I was stunned to see and hear them zipping around us. I was trying to get attention to each Marine I heard, starting with Haug. I pressed on his wound and wrapped a bandage around his waist to secure the gauze and try to stop his bleeding. He kept firing and yelling, "Fall back," but nobody was falling back. I was still not totally sure what had happened during those first few minutes of the firefight, but I knew I only heard a few guys crying out, or firing their M-16s and tossing grenades toward the enemy position. I looked over to interpreter Kim and realized he was in very bad shape. In addition to having one of his legs almost blown off at the knee, he was blinded by the explosion. I think he might have been hit in his eyes, because he was bleeding from a head wound and holding his face near his eyes.

Ten minutes into the firefight, the enemy made their first charge at what was remaining of our platoon of sixteen. The first charge took out the two front Marines still fighting and wounded the second two Marines. They charged in groups of eight each of the three times they charged us, and the first two enemy charges towards us were suicide missions on their part. The two Marines who were wounded kept fighting. The third enemy charge got those two Marines killed right in front of me. They each took a round in the head, and one of the Marines was decapitated. Haug was still firing his weapon, and so was I. The adrenaline rush was the only thing keeping us fighting. All three of us were badly wounded as the third wave of enemy came out of the bush, attacking us on foot. They had sent about twenty-five NVA at us, and we had killed all of them as they charged. Haug told both of us to keep quiet. The radio had been destroyed in the initial blast, so we had no way to communicate with the TOC back on base. He wanted to let the enemy think they had wiped us out. It quickly became quiet, as there were no more rounds headed to the enemy from our position, and they couldn't hear anything.

After we waited quietly in pain for almost fifteen minutes, a group of about twenty enemy NVA came walking towards us. They shot into one of the forward Marines, apparently because he was still breathing. They spit on his corpse before they finished him off, and they did this several times as they walked closer towards us, looking for any sign of life on the ground. Haug whispered to me and Kim, "Load up your weapons. We're going to get the drop on these motherfuckers. Hold your fire until I start firing, but you make sure you fire that weapon, Kinane."

I said, "Don't worry about me. I've got eight full metal jackets, and I reload very fast." I knew this was our only chance, and I was ready to survive.

The enemy was out in the open, about ten yards in front of us, when Haug stood up and opened fire. We both started firing our M-16s at them, and we immediately dropped the first nine NVA in front. The NVA who didn't get hit with rounds lay down, and Haug said, "Come on, let's get them." Haug was firing in the ground at any sign of life from those first nine who had been hit by our rounds. The eleven on the ground quickly surrendered, holding up their arms and hands empty. Haug screamed at them, and they tossed their AK-47s, Brownings, and grenades behind them. It was at that moment, we realized Haug had been hit with another round again. This one in his left shoulder. The firing had stopped, and Haug told Kim to tell them to get on their feet. They were very scared and complied with Kim's order. Kim kept hollering at them from the ground. He couldn't walk, but he was lucid and engaged in what was happening. I remember thinking, *Thank God Kim's still okay*, because neither Haug nor I would have been able to communicate with these guys we were about to take prisoner.

Haug grabbed a very long rope from his gear and told Kim to have one of the NVA tie circles around each of his brother's necks. That guy was shaking like a leaf, and while Kim was barking in Vietnamese at him, he was already putting loops around each of the ten from his group. He finished, and Haug grabbed another rope from one our KIA Marines and started cutting the long rope into short pieces. He told Kim to tell that one NVA to tie the other's hands behind their backs. I kept my M-16 and .45 handgun pointed at them, trying to deal with my own minor pain, and blood dripping off my face. As the NVA finished tying his buddies up, Haug tied the last guy and attached him to the others by the loop around their necks. Haug told Kim to tell them they were now our prisoners, and if they fucking made any wrong move, we would waste them on the spot. Kim yelled at them, and they nodded in agreement, except one guy, who didn't say anything and looked very upset about being tied up and taken prisoner. He worried me, and he seemed to be the hard-core NVA leader.

Haug told them to sit down, and they all sat down at the same time. Haug sat down too and told me to keep an eye on them. He was badly injured and quietly told me he didn't know how long it would be before he passed out. He told me, just in case, I should follow the path back towards Charlie Med, which was probably two miles away. Before we got up, we drank and emptied one of my three canteens. I asked Haug if I could toss one of the two canteens I had left to the enemy, because they were a mess too, and looked thirsty as we drank our water. Haug at first said, "No fucking way, Kinane. These motherfuckers just wasted thirteen Marines, and maybe this one if we don't get back to base. Kim may not make it either."

I said, "This may be a small peace offering, Sergeant."

Just then, Haug's eyes rolled up, and he lay back on the ground with a deep grunt. He didn't pass out, but he was in bad shape as he kept his M-16 pointed at the prisoners. Haug was on the ground on my right, and Kim was in pain on the ground to my left.

While taking a minute trying to let Haug and Kim rest and recover enough to start walking out of the bush with these prisoners, I could hear the two prisoners who didn't seem willing to comply talking to the others. Kim motioned for me to lean towards his face. I could barely hear him, but he was trying to tell me something important. He was bleeding a lot, and said, "They're planning to overtake you and Sergeant Haug. They've all just agreed not to be taken prisoner." I looked back at them talking among themselves and realized what Kim had just told me.

I stood up, without any hesitation, and fired a full jacket from my M-16 and reloaded to finish all eleven of them off. I figured it was us or them, and I was the only one at that moment who was able to get up and fire. I killed each one and left them exactly where they fell, with all the ropes on them. They had become too dangerous in my mind, because I wasn't sure I wouldn't pass out soon as well. I walked back to Haug and Kim, and I could hear Haug say, "Good job, Kinane. Get me on my feet, and let's get the fuck back to base."

Kim wasn't walking, so I realized I would have to carry him on my shoulders. I pulled him up and started carrying him behind a limping Haug. We were all bleeding, and most of our clothes were either blown off of us or soaked with blood and sweat.

As we slowly moved the couple of miles back, we stopped about ten times to rest. Kim weighed only 115 pounds. It was easy carrying him, but I wasn't 100 percent, and I felt dizzy and weak. Haug stopped talking altogether, and the last two stops, it took him at least a half hour before he had strength to keep moving. We left the bush and could see the gate of the base. I tried to yell loud enough, trying not to drop Kim, who had already passed out, but he wasn't dead. Finally, when we got less than a klick away, they noticed us stumbling towards them. The gate immediately opened, and a jeep came charging toward us. When we realized we had made it, we all dropped to the ground. I had not realized how badly I had been wounded when I passed out. I could hear Haug talking as I lost consciousness.

From what I understand, they put us on the jeep and ran us back to the base, directly to the surgical bunker, where Pitt, Granato, Cranfit, Lynne, Martin, and Izzy were waiting for us. We were all in surgery at the same time, on different operating tables. They hooked us up to IVs and cut off our remaining clothes. They rolled us around on the table, trying to find all our wounds. I could tell I was being pulled around, but I couldn't figure out what was going on. I looked to my right, and Kim was saying something to Cranfit as she was attending to him. She was looking at him, and then she looked directly at me for a moment. Pitt was talking to Haug in the same manner, trying to get an assessment of what happened and where the others in the platoon were located. Haug was telling him everything, and twice during his conversation with Pitt, he pointed at me and spoke my name. I was in a fog, but I could tell they were talking about me, while they were struggling for their lives. I passed out.

I woke up in the recovery bunker. Haug was on the bed hooked up to an IV just like I was. He was sleeping from what I could tell. I asked for help, and a new corpsman I had never seen came up to me and said, "What do you need, Kinane?"

I said, "Water. Can I please have some water?"

"I can only give you chunks of ice."

"That would be great."

When he returned with a small cup with one cube of ice, I asked him where Kim was. He said, "Kim died on the operating table." I chewed on the ice and thought, *Damn*. Kim was such a good guy. All of those Marines who lost their lives that day were good guys. I looked at Haug and asked the corpsman how he was doing. He said, "You're both going to make it and get out of here. You're going to be transferred to Da Nang, and then to Manila. You're both in really bad shape, but soon you'll be stable enough to transport. You're probably out of here around 1500 today." He went on to say, "The base has been under heavy attack, and there are possibly hundreds of Marines at Khe Sanh about to arrive here at the same time. You'll be out of here in a couple hours. We've got all your personal gear, so you can take it with you."

Haug never woke up in front of me again, but I know he made it to Manila because I was right there with him. Before we left, Pitt, Granato, Lynne, and Martin came up to me and Pitt said, "You did a good job, Kinane. You'll be fine, and we'll miss you."

I said, "Thank you so much." I was on pain meds, so I wasn't totally lucid, but I could understand them and hear clearly what they were saying to me. Lt. Lynne and Lt. Martin leaned into me to say goodbye, and told me they had worked on me along with Lt. Commander Granato. They said, "Granato saved your life, Kinane." I looked at him, and tears started flowing down my face as I said, "Thank you so much, sir. Thank you so much, you guys. I'll never forget this."

Pitt was the last person to lean into me. "You'll be fine, Kinane. When you get a little better, you're going to be asked many questions in Manila, so be ready for those questions. We spoke with Staff Sergeant Haug before he passed out, and we spoke briefly with Kim before he passed away on the operating table," he said quietly.

Just then, my stretcher was moved by four Marines. Four Marines were also moving Haug at the same time. One from each stretcher was holding up our IV bottles while we walked toward a big Chinook helicopter waiting to take us to Da Nang. They had just dropped off forty fresh Marines, who were standing outside the main medical bunker, getting instructions. Haug and I were placed on the floor of the chopper, and it took off.

I do remember this. Almost as soon as we landed in Da Nang, we were transferred quickly to a C-130 and were quickly on our way to Manila. I remember thinking how lucky I was to be alive, wondering, *How did I survive this?*

HAUG AND I arrived at Naval Medical Center Manila and were placed in an ICU unit next to each other. After two days, I was moved to a different ward with about forty other guys. There were corpsmen and nurses everywhere. Most were Filipino. I thought, *This is definitely not the war zone anymore.* I was in that same ward room for the next two months, but a week after I got there, Haug arrived and began his recovery at the far end of the ward. We talked a little, but he wasn't strong and told me he wasn't supposed to be talking with me. I asked him why, and he said he just couldn't. "Orders," he said as he turned away to rest. I turned to walk back to my bed and wondered, *What the heck was that all about? Why couldn't he talk to me?*

About a week later, I figured out what was going on when a Navy lieutenant commander in full dress whites came up to my bed and told me he had news for me. I don't recall his name, but he was about thirty years old and sounded like he was from New York, or New England. I think his last name was Italian, but that's all I remember about him. He asked me whether I wanted the good news first or the bad news. I sat up on my bed and said, "Start with the good news."

He said, "You're being cited for a Congressional Medal of Honor."

I couldn't believe it, and then I remembered there was also bad news. I said, "And the bad news?"

He paused for a moment. "You're being charged with eleven counts of murder under the Geneva Convention rules of war."

"WHAT?!?" I couldn't believe what I had just heard. "What the fuck did I do?"

He said, "It was reported that you murdered eleven prisoners under your control when they were tied up."

Just then, it all came back to me. "This is bullshit. They were going to kill us as soon as Haug, Kim, and I passed out. I was defending myself, Haug, and Kim. Haug and I wouldn't be here if I didn't take action."

He said he wasn't able to talk too much and suggested that I not discuss this with anyone other than the Navy JAG (lawyer) officer who was being assigned to defend me. I lay back down and said, "Thank you, sir."

As he walked away, he said, "You must understand this now, Kinane. While you're recovering here, you're basically under arrest."

"Arrest?"

"Yes, but hang in there, Kinane. There's a side of this story I can't discuss with you now, but your JAG officer will fill you in completely. You're scheduled for a military court-martial in about a month, and it will take place here in Manila." As he was about to leave, he said, "Try to relax and get better,

Kinane. You're no longer in the war zone, and you're probably going to go home after this court-martial is over."

I laid my head back on my pillow and stared at the ceiling, thinking about what I was just told and about those eleven NVA who were plotting to kill me, Haug, and Kim out there in the bush. I just couldn't believe this was happening. Not after what had happened.

THREE DAYS LATER, a lady officer in full whites, with white skirt and shiny polished shoes, walked right up to my bed with a briefcase in her right hand. She introduced herself as my assigned Naval JAG officer and handed me her card. Her names was Krein, and the name tag on the front of her uniform confirmed her name. I looked at the card, as she said, "You're being charged with eleven counts of murder in the field, Kinane." I said I had heard that a couple of weeks ago from another officer. She said, "Yes, that would have been the officer working with the Navy inspector general. Don't talk to him anymore unless I'm with you. As a matter of fact, don't talk with anyone about this. Not even your friends back home, or even your family. Is that understood, Kinane?"

I said, "Yes ma'am, I understand." I looked at her card, and then the stripes on her shoulder boards and said, "You're a commander?"

She said, "Yes," as though I insulted her by being surprised. She went on to say, "I'm going to get you off these charges, Kinane, so you be very nice to me and keep your cool. I'll have you back home by this summer if you listen to me."

"Yes, Commander, and thank you."

"I will be visiting you each day, except on Sundays, until your court-martial trial is over, so keep your cool, and if anyone starts asking you questions, you show them my card and tell them in no uncertain terms only to talk to me, and that you have been ordered ONLY to discuss this case with me in the room." She looked at me and realized my incredulity. "You'll be fine, Kinane. You'll be fine. Don't be upset, and just get yourself well as soon as you can. I anticipate your court-martial to take place sometime in May this year. Get some rest, and I'll see you again soon." She turned around and walked out of the ward. I couldn't help thinking how pretty she was and how tough she seemed to be. I did notice an engagement diamond ring on her left hand. Some lucky guy was going to marry a beautiful and very smart Naval officer, and a lawyer, to boot.

I didn't sleep after hearing this news for at least thirty hours. I was shocked and stunned. Something wasn't right. What happened?

MAY 13, 1968 was a Monday, and I was in my full dress uniform being wheeled into my court-martial trial, with Commander Krein pushing my chair. At the front of the room were three judges in black robes sitting behind a table. There were chairs and benches facing the judges, and only about a dozen people watching. Commander Krein had told me quietly that every-thing was going to be okay... I said, "Gosh, I hope so," as I felt my body started to shake with a fear I had never ex-perienced. It was worse than the fear a few months ago in January, when I was in the bush. I was confused and hoping to God I wouldn't be found guilty of these charges. I didn't want to spend any time in prison for defending myself, trying to survive and stay alive. *Shit, I was in a war zone*, I thought. Commander Krein leaned into me and said, "Calm down, Kinane, you're going to be fine. Just calm down."

The middle judge was clearly running the show and in-troduced himself. He was a captain, and the two others were captains as well. They spoke in Latin terms to Krein and to the other officer at the table next to me. My name came up, and they asked me to try to stand so I could take an oath. I stood up slowly, raised my right hand, and repeated the oath. The middle judge told everyone to be seated. He started read-ing and talking about the incident between 0100 and 0400 on January 30, 1968 outside the perimeter of Charlie Med base outside Khe Sanh. He concluded by saying, "You have been cited by several officers to receive a Congressional Medal of Honor for your actions on that day. That's not going to hap-pen, Petty Officer Kinane, and I'm going to explain to you and Commander Krein why.

"A Navy nurse by the name of Lt. Cranfit reported that a Vietnamese interpreter, Phuc Mi Kim, told her you had mur-dered eleven prisoners under your control, and while they were tied up. She wrote a report, and we have had to address her report, because she spoke with a witness to the events be-fore he died during surgery at Charlie Med. She was the only person who said she heard Kim say this. Nobody else heard him say anything like that. If you don't already know, Staff Sergeant Haug passed away," he said.

I looked at Commander Krein to my right and said loudly to her, "Haug died? When?" As she tried to motion to me to be quiet and listen, the judge barked at me and told me not to ever interrupt him and to listen to my counselor. I said, "Sorry, sir. Yes, sir."

He continued. "Several people had interviewed Staff Sergeant Haug, a combat-decorated Marine, before he passed away from his wounds. He repeated the story you have told us. He said interpreter Kim had told you that your prisoners were aware of your conditions while they were in ropes, and that they were conspiring to kill you, Haug, and Kim as soon as you passed out, and that you took action with your M-16 to stop this obvious threat. You did not execute them. You killed the enemy. Had you taken your .45 out and fired a bullet into their heads, I would consider that execution, but you did not. You used your M-16, and we have evidence to support this, and Haug confirmed this story at least five times while here before he died.

"It's my understanding Navy nurse Lt. Cranfit made up this report on you, which could never be collaborated by anyone else. Kim died right after talking with her, while he was about to have surgery. He died of his wounds. It was reported after you were demobilized out of Vietnam that Lt. Cranfit was stealing controlled narcotics from the Charlie Med medical supplies, and was caught by Commander Pitt, and his XO, Lt. Commander Granato. They found her passed out with a needle in her arm after she had injected morphine. It has been reported that when she woke up, she was told that she was under arrest for theft of narcotics and drug abuse on base. After being read the charges against her by Commander Pitt, she walked out of the room and grabbed a Marine's sidearm and shot herself in the head, committing suicide. Lt. Cranfit is dead. Her report bears no merit in this court, and we have concluded you did not execute these prisoners, because they were plotting to kill you as soon as you passed out. This is what we believe happened, and this is what the record will show. Furthermore, you will receive a Silver Star for your bravery, and not a CMH. You will receive a second Purple Heart for the wounds you are currently recovering from due to that combat action. You will also receive a Combat Medical Badge, and as soon as you finish recovering back home at Great Lakes Naval Medical hospital, where I once worked for three years as a surgeon, you will receive an Honorable Discharge. Your day of discharge will be based on your health and recovery back home in Illinois."

Commander Krein was looking at me as I started to understand what had happened, and what was going to happen. I let out a big sigh of relief, and Commander Krein patted me on the back. "I told you, you would be fine, Kinane."

The middle judge said, "This court-martial hearing is done, and let the record stand." They got up and left the room in a single file.

EARLY THAT JUNE in 1968, I got on a Navy C-130 headed back to the States, and the Great Lakes. We landed at Glenview

Naval Air Base in Illinois on June 8. It was a beautiful Saturday around sunset, and I got into a bus with my wheelchair and headed to Great Lakes Naval Hospital north of Glenview.

On June 29, 1968, I received my Honorable Discharge (DD-214).

I LOOKED UP at J.D. and his crew listening to my long story, and I said, "That's about all I can remember, J.D., and this is my DD-214 to prove it." I held it up in front of my chest for the camera.

J.D. said, "Cut," and everyone in the room took a deep breath. J.D. said, "That's amazing, Uncle Charlie. I had heard some stories during some of the holidays from your brother, my grandpa, but I know you've never really spoken about what happened. Thank you so much for these last few hours." As I was slowly getting up from my chair, J.D. said, "Do you need a ride anywhere? I know you have your retirement party today, and I think you said you also had a V.A. health care appointment."

I said, "I've got a ride, and yes, I'm retiring from the bench today. It's time, and this diabetes is not helping me lately. That's why I'm back at the V.A. later today."

J.D. asked me how long I had been a judge, and I told him I became a federal judge seven years after my brother became one, so that would make it almost twenty-five years now. I looked at all these college kids in the room and said, "Thanks, you guys," and started for the elevator down the hall. I'd never have to discuss that time again, because my nephew J.D. had it all on tape. I hoped he would get a good grade. The elevator door closed to go down to the street and I got into my car.

THE END.